ALSO BY ALEX CAGE

Orlando Black Series

Carolina Dance (Novel)

Queen City Ruby (Short Story)

Sunshine Scandal (Short Story)

Once You Go Black (Short Story)

Bayside Boom (Novel)

Family Famous (Novella)

Leroy Silver Series

Contracts & Bullets

Aloha & Bullets

Get the latest releases and exclusive giveaways, sign up to the Alex Cage Reader List.

www.AlexCage.com/signup

THE WAR BACK HOME

ALEX CAGE

JOIN THE READER'S LIST

Get the latest releases and exclusive giveaways - sign up to the Alex Cage Reader List:

www.AlexCage.com/signup

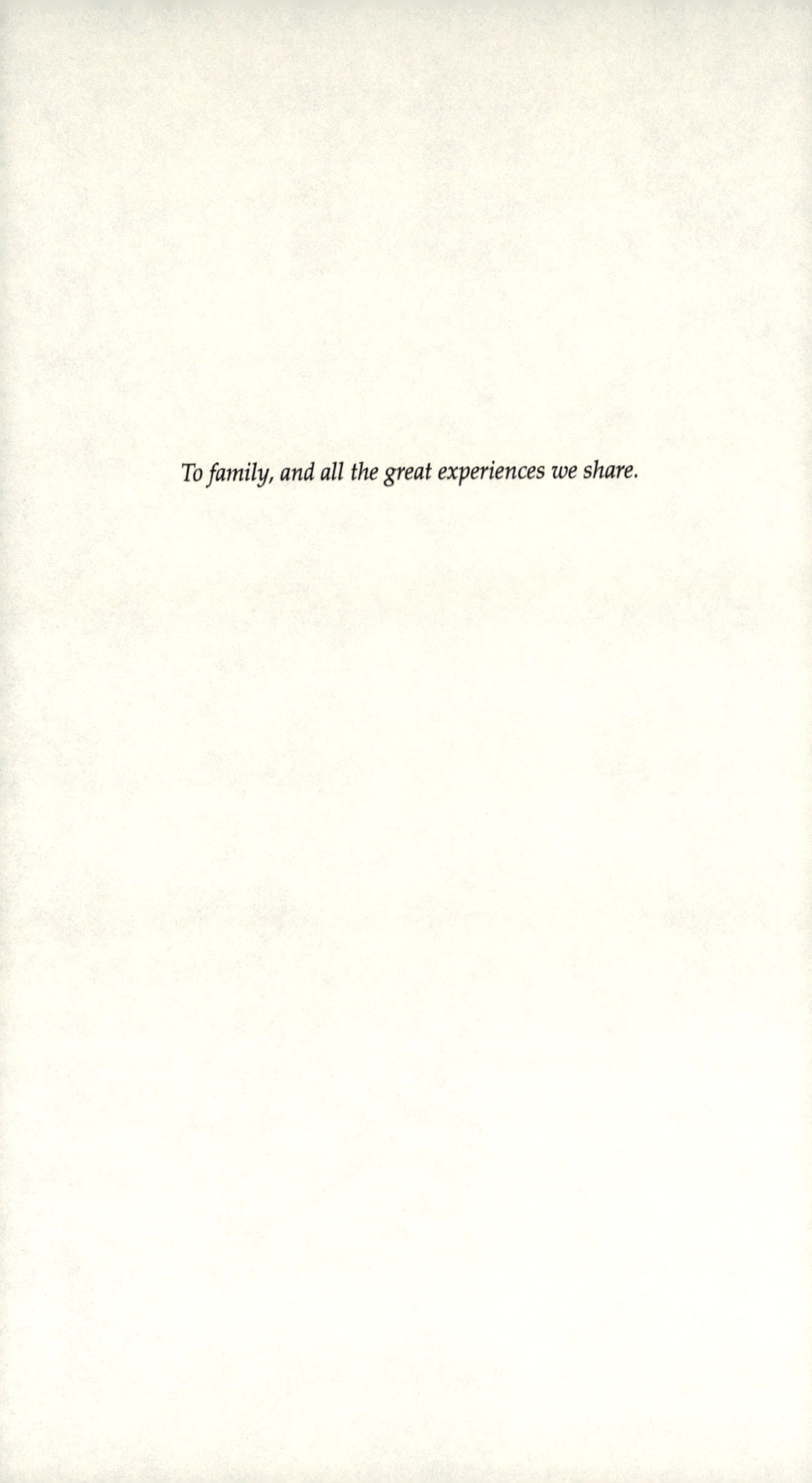

To family, and all the great experiences we share.

THE WAR BACK HOME

CHAPTER
ONE

The late afternoon sun beamed down on Clarence Tucker as he passed through the village. His fatigue pants were covered with dusty sand and his shirt was drenched in sweat. He wiped the perspiration from his forehead as he walked through a shaded alley between two mud houses. At the center of the village, the smell of spices wafted in the air, and a group of kids were kicking a ball. They cheered and high-fived Tucker as he walked by. He waved bye to the kids and continued toward the gated area where he shared a cabin with his close friend Pozo and two other A-team members from his unit, Manny and John. When Tucker entered, he saw Manny and John playing cards on Manny's lower bunk bed.

"Yo, wanna play?" Manny asked, flashing his gold tooth through a crooked smile.

"Nah, got to take a shower. Where's Pozo?"

"What, he ain't tied to ya apron strings?" Manny said.

John laughed, and Tucker just smiled and started stripping.

Pozo entered the cabin as Tucker stepped out of his pants.

"Mamma Mia, lookie that bum," Pozo said, grinning as he used his rifle to tap Tucker's bum.

"Man, get out of here, weirdo," Manny said, wrinkling his nose.

"Captain America would beg to have this butt, bruh."

"Get lost, freak," Tucker said, laughing as he walked out of the cabin and to the bath area.

Pozo was the goofball of the group, but well loved by the villagers and gained the village chief's trust before anyone else in the unit.

After taking a shower, Tucker returned to the cabin and found Pozo alone.

"Where's the others?"

"Dinner. Manny said he couldn't wait any longer for you to get done with your lady bath."

Tucker narrowed his eyes.

Pozo laughed, his hands up in a surrender pose. "Amigo, his words, not mine."

Tucker lay down on his own bed after toweling off, reminiscing about the day's events.

"You know, I'm going to miss this little village," Pozo said while lying on his back in his bed, legs up and crossed.

"Yeah? Why?"

"Are you seriously asking me that?" Pozo said before sitting up. "I mean, this is the most peaceful deployment we've ever had. Apart from those pesky little insurgents, our guerrilla forces have been able to contain on their own. We've had nothing to do except psyops."

"True, but this is also our eighth deployment as a team in Iran, and I have to tell you, I am tired, man. We've been here for a minute and I gotta say, when Cap mentioned he thought we'd be pulled out three weeks from now, it was the happiest I've felt in years," Tucker said.

Pozo laughed. "Man, I get you, but still, I'm gonna miss 'em. You will too, if you're being honest. Especially that lady friend of yours," Pozo said while laughing in his usual maniacal manner.

"What lady friend? Bruh, come off that." Tucker scoffed.

Pozo laughed and went back to reading.

"You've been reading this book for how long now, Spanish?"

"For as long as you've had your lady friend."

Tucker chuckled. "Seriously man, whatchu gonna do when we get back home?" he asked.

Pozo put down his book and grinned, rubbing his wide palms together.

"First, Imma eat a year's supply of hamburgers."

"Serious, Alejandro," Tucker said, knowing that Pozo disliked being called by that name.

Pozo snarled at him. "Don't call me that, black kid."

Tucker laughed. "Talk, Alejandro."

"I'm just gonna ignore your insolence to a superior officer and answer your question."

Tucker shook his head. He was a sergeant first class and Pozo was a staff sergeant, but that was apparently irrelevant to Pozo.

"So, black kid, after eating a year's worth of hamburgers, I'll retire to my grandma's basement and catch up on my gaming. Manny plans to go into private security, but like the Indians say, not my circus, not my monkeys." Then he cocked an eyebrow. "Or is it the Polish who says that?" He shrugged and Tucker chuckled.

"So, you're just gonna eat hamburgers and play games?"

"Yep," Pozo replied, straightfaced.

Tucker studied his face. "Man, you really are serious."

"You thought I was joking? Why do you think I call my grandma so much? Think it's cos I love her? Okay," he said after a crooked smile, "I actually love her, but I've been calling her with instructions on building my man cave. Imma get me the latest console the market has to offer, and then I'm off."

"Man, you're crazy," Tucker said after a moment of staring at his friend.

"That's why we're pals, bro. Why else would a black kid and a not-so-white kid become best friends in the military?"

Tucker waved him off, grinning. Pozo got up from his bed and wagged his bum in front of Tucker before dancing away toward the back of the cabin. A moment later, he was back, dressed in a faded shirt and his uniform pants. He slipped a grenade into his pocket on both sides.

Tucker stared at him.

"Can't be too careful," Pozo said. "Let's get something to eat. I'm starving," he continued while prancing around the cabin, waiting for Tucker to get ready.

"Alright, let's go," Tucker said, dressed in some fresh army pants and a blue tank top.

"Speaking of which, bruh, what do you plan on doing when we get back to the States?"

"I don't know, man," Tucker said as they walked from the army's cabins and out of the gated area. Tucker loved the evening in Ashibar. The air was normally cool and it caressed the skin lightly, a great relief from the afternoon when the sun beat down mercilessly on the Iranian village like a vengeful creditor beating on the door of a longtime debtor.

It could get so bad that it felt like the moisture was being sucked from the skin. But what the village lacked in good afternoon weather, it more than made up for in great hospitality regardless of the time of the day.

A little girl ran up to Pozo, and he gave her a high five. Delighted, she danced back to her mother.

Tucker smiled. "You'd make a great father, Pozo," he said, knowing it would annoy him.

"What? Don't ever tell me that crap again. Father? You want me to be in charge of another human being for the rest of my life? Me? In charge of an actual human with bones, teeth, flesh and hair? Nah, stop it bruh."

"But you'd be great at it, Pozo."

"Man, shut up."

Tucker chuckled.

"And by the way, I'm not eating that funny stuff you had me eat yesterday."

"It was meat, Alejandro. Goat meat," Tucker said, drawing out every word like he was talking to a child. Pozo ignored him, and Tucker laughed when he realized he wouldn't get a rise out of him.

"Whatever. I'm not interested," Pozo said.

"Alright, Spaniard. What would you like?"

"An American hamburger, but when do I ever get what I want?"

Manny and John approached, laughing at some private joke.

"Hey look Manny, it's Black-eo and Foo-liet," John said, and both men laughed again.

"Ha-ha, very funny," Pozo said while feinting to hit Manny.

Manny scurried away, and John stepped back.

"See, they scared of these fists," Pozo said, gesticulating in the manner of a boxer. A few locals watching laughed and clapped, and after his demonstrations, Pozo curtsied and ambled away.

They arrived at the central market of the village. As usual, the market was bubbling with activity. Tucker observed the happenings from a slightly aloof standpoint, but Pozo was the opposite. Tucker watched as his friend mixed in with the locals. The people fully accepted, loved, and respected the special forces team as protectors and guides.

A guerrilla forces battalion leader approached Tucker. He wore fatigues and a turban. *What was his name?* Tucker tried to remember. Adnan, he recalled.

"How has your day been, soldier?" Adnan asked in Arabic.

"Fine, thank you," Tucker replied in Arabic. "Tiring, but it's been fine. Yours?"

"Tiring too. Some of the boys in training with my battalion got into a fight, and I had to separate them. Very annoying."

Tucker smiled. "That's going to happen sometimes. You just have to tighten up on the discipline. They'll be fine," Tucker said.

"Thank you, Ismail," the guerrilla soldier said, and after a few moments, he walked away. *Ismail?* Tucker momentarily forgot the name given to him by the village chief after he saved his daughter from two men who attempted to rape her.

"Hey, where'd you go?" Pozo said as he approached Tucker, holding a stick with large chunks of meat.

"What are you eating, Pozo?"

Pozo glanced at the meat briefly. "Meat."

Tucker smiled. "I think that's goat meat."

Pozo inspected the meat for a few seconds, shrugged, and took a bite.

"Don't blame me if you get constipated," Tucker warned.

Pozo smiled and motioned toward Tucker's back.

Tucker turned and saw the village chief's daughter, Dana.

"Hi," she greeted.

Tucker smiled.

"Wait, you speak English now?" Pozo asked.

She nodded and smiled.

"Nothing too fancy," Tucker said. "And keep that quiet, will you? I don't know how her dad will take it."

"He like Americans," she said.

Tucker's eyes widened. "Really?" he asked.

She nodded with a smile. "And he wants to give Pozo an honorary title, though he won't tell anybody which," she said in Arabic before winking.

The three of them laughed.

Dana looked at Tucker and grinned. "Madam Khodija said to tell you thank you for your recipe. It has been a big hit with her customers," she said. "And she mentioned your meals next week are on her."

"Hear that, Pozo? Volunteering at a restaurant really works, don't it? A week's worth of free food!" Tucker said in Arabic.

Dana laughed.

"Well, you know you gotta take your pal," Pozo said.

"Scram!" Tucker told him.

Pozo was about to reply when a loud explosion shook the village.

CHAPTER
TWO

Screams echoed throughout the village as the locals scattered and took cover near their homes.

Tucker and Pozo barreled toward the cabins.

They got their gear and raced to the first cabin, where the detachment officer, Declan, was busy barking orders.

"Eighteen foxtrot, give me updates!" he shouted into his radio.

"Cap, a small band of insurgents just attacked the chief's house and has killed him and taken the rest of his family hostage," the soldier reported back through the radio.

"Oh, no…" Declan said on a sigh.

"We're outside with the guerilla forces. They want blood."

"Okay, keep them calm long enough till the rest of us arrive. Over."

"Over."

"Wade, I want you and Rash there ASAP. Our priority is the chief's family, but attend to anyone who's injured," Declan shouted into the radio.

He turned to Tucker and Pozo. "I want you guys there now, on the double. Comb the area for any insurgents and ensure the guerilla forces are armed as necessary. I'm right behind you."

Tucker and Pozo nodded, then raced out of the cabin.

Pozo tilted his head toward his shoulder radio. "Eighteen foxtrot, we're approaching from the west side of the building. Are we clear to proceed?" Pozo asked Daniel, the eighteen foxtrot.

"Negative, negative. A shootout has started. More insurgents are pouring out, and this'll turn into a bloodbath soon. Proceed from the east side and watch your six."

"These bastards," Pozo seethed. "I thought we had got them all."

Tucker was calm, deadly calm. "We'll get them all. We'll finish this today."

The two approached the building, cautiously scanning the environment for threats before slipping inside the compound unnoticed.

"Eighteen foxtrot, we're inside the compound. Repeat, we are in the compound," Tucker said into his radio.

"Get to the west side of the main building. Eighteen Charlie is there waiting. Blow the door open and get inside. We'll take care of the ones outside."

After receiving their orders, Tucker and Pozo moved in, like lions creeping up on their prey.

"Pozo, I count six insurgents. I can take out four of them."

Pozo's face was a mask of anger fused with concentration. "I'll take care of the other two."

Tucker nodded and counted down from three with his fingers before springing out from hiding and stabbing the first insurgent in the neck. He yanked the man's body in front of himself and used him as a human shield, albeit a dead one. The insurgent's body jerked violently as a brief rain of bullets pierced it. Tucker threw a knife with a flex of his wrist, burying the blade in the shooter's neck.

He dropped a third insurgent with a shot to the head and pushed the fourth against a wall.

"Where's the rest of your team?" he bellowed in Arabic. The insurgent grinned, and Tucker slapped him.

"I'll ask you just once more. Where's the rest of your team?" he yelled again in Arabic. The insurgent kept grinning, and Tucker held his neck and plunged a knife into his stomach.

"Waste of youth," Pozo said before kicking the dead body.

"Eighteen foxtrot, we're clear in the entrance alley," Tucker said into his radio.

In that moment, a shot rang over Tucker's head and he ducked for cover.

"We are not clear!" he shouted into the radio again. "I repeat, we are not clear!"

"Stay clear of the doors," Daniel's voice scratched through the speaker. "Eighteen Charlie is here and setting charges. Tell me when you're clear of the blast zone."

"Pozo, get away from the doors. They're gonna blow it open," Tucker yelled.

Pozo moved behind a beam. "We're clear," Tucker said into the radio.

"Roger that."

A second later, the doors to the entrance alley of the chief's house erupted into chunks of wood. Adnan was the first to dash inside, and his battalion of twenty followed. The remaining members of the A-team followed suit.

"I'm sorry," Tucker said to Adnan.

The battalion leader nodded, with tears in his eyes and rage on his face.

"Report!" Declan barked.

"There's some shooters in the area above, and the doors to the main building are locked from within," Pozo said.

"Manny, blow these doors!" Declan directed, and Manny

charged the door with feverish excitement. A few moments later, the door was no more.

"Hold!" Declan shouted, and just in time. The remaining insurgents inside opened fire and the soldiers and guerilla forces in the entrance alley ducked for cover.

Snarling, Pozo pulled the pins on two grenades and tossed them into the passage. Twin explosions rang, and the shooting stopped. "Adnan, go!"

The leader of the guerilla forces didn't need a second invitation. He charged into the dust with his battalion.

"Charlie and Echo, stay here and watch the perimeter," Declan directed. "Zulu, Foxtrot, Delta and Bravo, you're with me."

The special forces members quickly went to the front of the lines, and Declan held up a fist. All movements ceased immediately.

"I know you have come for us, and we are not afraid to die," a voice said from the darkness. "But before we go, we will give the village chief's family the same punishment he has gotten. He stole the government from us, but now we will make sure no one from his family has it." The voice continued, "Before we execute his family, we will read his crimes to your hearing. His first crime is accepting to live in this house that the corrupt American government built for him after helping him steal the government from us."

As the voice continued reading the alleged crimes of the dead village chief, Tucker found his way to Declan.

"I can get to the family. They are most likely being held in the upper chamber beside the prayer room. That's the biggest room in the house," he said.

Declan looked at him with squinted eyes. "Roy, what do you think?" he asked the detachment technician.

"I say let him go. He knows the house well," Roy said.

"So does the guerilla forces."

"But they don't have his tactical training, do they?"

"Look, we're wasting time here. Either he goes in or not, decide," Joseph, the team daddy, said.

Declan pursed his lips and shook his head. "Okay go," he said. "Take Pozo with you."

Tucker and Pozo went out of the building and around the back. As they left the alley, gunshot blasts stuffed the sky. Tucker knew the team could hold their own, but he wasn't sure about the guerilla forces, as this was their first battle.

"Hold," Tucker said.

Pozo stopped.

"There's an army of these insurgents here."

Pozo frowned. "Where do they keep coming from?"

"Beats me," Silver clicked on his radio. "Eighteen foxtrot, come in."

The line scratched as Daniel's voice came through. "Go."

"There's a number of insurgents here and we're going to need a coordinated assault to bring them down."

"How many?"

Tucker's eyes roamed over the insurgents. "I count thirty-seven."

"Confirm count."

Tucker counted again. "Thirty-seven, confirmed."

"Wait for backup."

"Negative. We've wasted enough time," Tucker said and clicked off the radio.

"You know you'll get in trouble for that, right?" Pozo asked as he laid down his grenades.

"I'll deal with that later," Tucker said, his eyes fixed on the insurgents.

"I have six grenades here."

"Make that twelve," Tucker said and laid out his grenades too.

"Okay, Pozo, this is how it's going to go. You draw their fire, and I'll infiltrate the building from the back. I'll come back for you."

Pozo held his gaze. "There's thirty-seven men, Tucker. Not even I can take on that much."

"You don't need to. Take out as many as you can, Pozo. You grew up on a farm, the woods are your habitat. Use the trees to your advantage," Tucker said.

Pozo nodded grimly and gathered up nine of the grenades.

Tucker smiled and raised his hand up, counting from three to zero.

They both slung a grenade each, and two simultaneous blasts rocked the waiting band of insurgents, and gunfire rang out.

Weaving in between trees, Tucker aimed a grenade at a small group of insurgents who were standing close together. A blast later, different body parts of all five men scattered in various directions.

"One more shot," Tucker said to himself, gripping his last grenade tightly.

"Pozo!" he screamed and ran from where he was to behind another tree. Bullets beat upon the tree, but Tucker knew he was safe behind it.

Three concurrent blasts slaughtered over ten men, and Pozo yelled from somewhere in the forest.

"Last man standing!"

Tucker brought his assault rifle to bear and readied himself for the approaching insurgents.

"Three, two, one, go," he whispered, and when he hit go, he stepped out from behind the tree and fired.

The fury of bullets from his rifle caught two insurgents. Tucker dove into a small ditch behind a fallen log for cover. When he peeked over the log and looked beyond the fence surrounding the village chief's home, he saw a large blast hole in the side of the house. It was a point of access for him, but three insurgents stood in the way.

"Come out and surrender," the insurgents said in Arabic as they inched towards his position.

Tucker looked at the grenade in his hand. If he pulled the pin and threw it, it would kill the three men, but they were too close, so it could kill him as well.

Tucker was about to stand when three shots rang almost simultaneously, followed by three dull thuds from bodies hitting the ground.

"Saved you again," Pozo said with a grin.

Tucker laughed, and both of them jogged toward the house. Gunshots were still ringing and Tucker knew time would soon run out for the family.

"Pozo, take the right. I'll take the left. With all that ruckus out there, I don't think they heard anything, so we might still have the element of surprise, and we—"

A radio that was in the hands of a dead insurgent cut Tucker short.

"Prep the hostages for execution. We can't hold them any longer!" an insurgent screamed in Arabic.

"They're gonna kill them! Go!" Tucker said while grabbing a low hanging tree branch. He made a quick climb up the tree and vaulted over the fence. He and Pozo landed within seconds of each other and sprinted through the blast hole in the side of the house, then upstairs.

"Die, American devils!" an insurgent screamed as he lobbed a grenade at them. Tucker and Pozo dove in separate directions to avoid the grenade. Seconds later, a blast blew a huge chunk from one of the house's support beams.

Tucker shot the insurgent. "Another explosion like that and this place is gonna go down," he told Pozo.

The insurgent's radio scratched. "Are the hostages ready for execution?" a voice said in Arabic.

"We better hurry," Tucker said.

Tucker and Pozo raced to the upper chamber beside the prayer room. Two distinct voices shouted orders from inside the room. Tucker leaned against the wall, peeked inside, and saw two insurgents with their rifles aimed at the group of hostages. Tucker looked at Pozo while pointing at his own eyes, then the room before holding up two fingers.

Pozo nodded and Tucker gestured for them to ease back down the hall. When they were at a safe distance, Tucker removed two throwing knives.

"Two enemies and three hostages," he whispered. "I didn't see any radios, so I don't believe the insurgents received the kill order yet."

"Yeah, I think the one we just killed was supposed to deliver the message to them," Pozo said.

"Probably, but either way, we may have to give up our guns as a play to keep the hostages safe. Take this." Tucker handed Pozo one knife. "These are my last two, so don't miss."

"I got this, bro," Pozo said.

"Okay, let's move."

"Roger that."

The two crept back to the door. They looked at one another and quickly nodded before Pozo zipped to the opposite side of the doorway. Immediately voices shouted from inside the room and four blasts stuffed the area.

Tucker and Pozo leaned away and ducked as the hostages screamed and debris flung from the door frame.

One insurgent shouted over the cries of the hostages. "We will kill them!" he yelled. "Drop your weapons and come out!"

"Okay, we're dropping our weapons!" Tucker said while peeking into the room.

There was an insurgent close to the back with his gun trained on the hostages. He stood on the right side of the room next to a window. The other insurgent stood near the front, close to Tucker's side, with his gun aimed at the doorway.

Tucker looked at Pozo and pointed at the door. "I'll take the one on my side," he mouthed.

"Now!" the insurgent close to the door yelled. "Drop them now and come out!"

Tucker and Pozo dropped their guns and showed their hands. Pozo entered the room first, then Tucker.

Tucker knew they had less than ten seconds before the insurgents decided to either shoot him and Pozo or take them as hostages, so he kept his eyes on both insurgents and looked for an opportunity. A moment later, he had one. The insurgent near the back took his attention off the hostages and moved his gun away from them. Pozo noticed and reached for his knife. The other insurgent, close to Tucker, saw Pozo's movements and began swinging his aim at Pozo. Before the man could get a lock on Pozo, Tucker threw his knife and pierced the insurgent's neck. The man dropped his gun and reached for his neck before falling back.

By that time, Pozo had flung his knife at the insurgent near the hostages. The knife punctured the man's shoulder. He stumbled back but kept hold of his gun.

"Argh, I wanted the neck!" Pozo said.

Tucker bolted toward the insurgent and tackled him before the terrorist could bring his gun to bear.

"Watch the window!" Pozo yelled.

Glass shattered and Tucker's body arched outside the window as his feet left the floor. He quickly grabbed the outside window ledge and watched as the insurgent clawed, flopped, and screamed before smacking into the ground.

As Tucker heaved himself toward the window, his elbow slipped.

"Gotcha!" Pozo said while grabbing the back of Tucker's vest and pulling him up. "Man, you weigh a ton."

Tucker grinned. "Must be my head."

Pozo grunted as he dragged him up and into the room. The two turned to find the hostages staring at them.

"Everyone's okay?" Tucker asked.

They nodded.

"Awesome," Tucker said as he took a seat on the floor.

Pozo joined him, and they sat shoulder to shoulder, panting.

"I think I owe you one," Pozo said.

"No, I think we're even," Tucker said. "If it wasn't for you, I might be a pancake right now. Thanks."

"Anytime, amigo."

The death of the village chief sent shock waves through the village, and in the following days, there was a general sadness among the locals.

"We're still being recalled, right?" Tucker asked Pozo a couple of days after the incident.

"Yeah, I think. Declan mentioned to Joseph, who mentioned to me that top brass is satisfied with the work we've done, especially with training the guerilla forces and their subsequent decisive participation in the clash with the insurgents."

"Great. I admit I'll miss these people, but I miss home more."

"Yep," Pozo agreed.

The locals threw a party for the team the day they left, and while the other team members were having fun at the party, Tucker was with Dana.

"I don't want you to go. Can't you tell your bosses you want to stay?" she pleaded in Arabic.

Tucker shook his head. "It's not possible," he said. "Also, I need to see my mom. I haven't seen her since my dad died."

Dana nodded.

"Will you come back?"

Tucker hung his head. "Dana, I don't know. All I know is that I'll never forget your kindness, both to me and to my team."

"And our village will never forget your legendary cooking skills," she said with a smile. "I remember the first day I ate your food. I told my mother it was the best food I had ever eaten, and she sent me to my room in annoyance. The next day, I saw her talking to you about the recipe," she reminisced.

Tucker laughed. He remembered that day, too.

"Tucker," she began in English, making Tucker's brows rise. "I will miss you."

Tucker smiled. "I'll miss you too."

"Will you cook when you get to America?" she asked, switching back to Arabic.

"I don't know. Maybe I will."

Dana was about to say something when Pozo hollered at Tucker. "Pal, ride's here."

"It's time," Dana said.

Tucker nodded.

"Take care, and may we meet again," she said while standing.

"Will you do something for me?" Tucker asked in Arabic.

"Anything," she said in a soft tone.

"Give Adnan some attention," he said before moving closer to her and whispering, "I think he likes you."

Dana laughed and nodded. "We'll see. Goodbye, Tucker," she said as he walked toward Pozo.

CHAPTER
THREE

Tucker's smile from something Pozo said disappeared the moment he walked down the stairs of the plane. *It was good to be home*, he thought. But it was better to have those who cared welcome you home, he considered as he watched his colleagues with their mothers and fathers and wives and children and brothers. He greeted Pozo's grandma, but that was all he could manage before disappearing.

His destination was the same place he had left; an apartment in downtown New York, one he had kept since he was a student. From the day he moved into the apartment, Tucker felt a resonance in his heart, like he had found the place made just for him. Not like the apartment was special or even looked like much, but it was the biggest unit in the complex and he had practically threatened his landlord, Royce, to get it. After Tucker mentioned he'd tell Royce's wife that the married man and father of two was hitting on a student named Shirley, the landlord was more than eager to negotiate a lease agreement with Tucker for the apartment unit. Tucker chuckled at the thought of it all.

The smile on his face as he reminisced quickly disappeared as another thought plagued his mind. Would he ever be satisfied with one woman? Would he catch the womanizer bug? He chuckled again. His own private thoughts were definitely amusing him.

An airport taxi stopped beside him as soon as he stepped out with his wheeled box. A middle-aged man with a sunny smile came out in a hurry and greeted him.

"Hello, Officer. Welcome home. May I get your luggage?"

Tucker nodded and passed his box to the man. He was short. He stopped just at Tucker's chest and had to look high to speak to Tucker. When he was sure his luggage was safe, Tucker got in the backseat and pulled the seat belt.

"Downtown New York," he said to the driver, who smiled again.

They drove for about three minutes in silence, and Tucker felt a slight thud in his chest. Even though he had no one waiting for him at home, he was eager to sleep in his own bed again. From the mirror, he noticed the driver stealing a glance at him for the fourth time, by his count.

Annoyed at the staring, Tucker blurted, "Can I help you with something?"

The driver's smile irritated him. *What was funny anyway?*

"I'm sorry, kind sir," the man said, still smiling sheepishly. Tucker thought he really looked like a sheep at that moment.

"Can I help you with something" Tucker repeated his question, but this time with a firmer tone.

"Yes," the man replied.

"What is it then?" Tucker snapped.

The driver sighed and raised his brows. "My daughter is in love with a soldier like you, and I'm really confused."

Tucker scoffed. *What now?* "What's your confusion?" He had become a little less irritated.

"What she'd do with herself when he's away at war? Long days, months, even years?"

"So, are you saying soldiers shouldn't have a family?" Tucker cut in.

The man raised his hand quickly. "No, sir, that's not what I'm saying. But she'll be lonely."

"Allow her to make her own choices, don't you think?"

"I'm trying to guide her, sir…"

"How old is she?" Tucker cut in again. He knew he was intimidating the man, and he enjoyed it. Anyone who thought soldiers should not have a family ought to be made to go through some orientation prison. Yeah, because that was not a great way to reward people who risked their lives to keep the country safe.

"She's twenty-four," the man answered.

"What's your name?" Tucker asked.

"Anthony, sir."

"Look, I assume a Twenty-four-year-old woman is old enough to decide for herself. And soldiers deserve to get married. So, let her, would you?"

They came to a traffic light and Anthony stopped to wait for the green light. He turned to look back at Tucker.

"Do you have a family?" he asked.

"I hope to," Tucker said.

Anthony turned back around. A frown had replaced his smile, and Tucker felt sorry for him.

"No matter how you feel, you can't make her choices for her. And there's no case here, except you don't think he's good enough for your daughter."

Anthony nodded continuously and Tucker wondered which of the things he said he agreed with.

Twenty minutes later, they were in downtown New York, and Anthony parked the taxi near the curb.

"I'll get your luggage," he said as they both exited the car. "Thank you for the advice, sir," he said, handing the luggage to Tucker.

"Well, thank you for your services," Tucker said while pulling a few bucks from his pocket. "Here's your pay, plus extra."

Anthony waved the money away. "I was going to tell you I'd do this for free," he said.

Tucker knitted his eyebrows. "Why?" he asked.

"You deserve more. I don't know what war you're coming from, but you deserve more for all the sacrifice."

Tucker smiled. He felt that was a kind thing to say. "Thank you, Anthony," he said before shaking the driver's hand.

Downtown New York was as lively as Tucker remembered. He was glad to be back to the noise of children playing football in the park. The sky looked different here. He supposed it was because it was a peaceful zone. Peace. That was a word he longed for since the war. And now that he had it, he was grateful.

He took the stairs up to his apartment with certainty. He definitely missed what was a normal life. Although a part of him worried about what he'd do with himself now that he was ex-military, he also knew this was what he wanted to do. *Totally.* After fighting all his life, maybe this was the time to experience some freshness and eat some good food. *And find some love?* His mind teased him. "Nah," he said to himself in Officer Rowney's voice. He'd experience freshness, eat good food he made, and have a good life, love or not.

When he knocked on his apartment's door, Rosie, a friend from his youth, opened it as he expected. He had arranged with her to stay there till he returned from his official duties and called her some days ago to let her know he was returning.

Rosie threw her arms around his neck, almost making him trip.

"Hey, Rosie," he said, allowing her to hold on for as long as she wanted. Not that it made any difference to him.

"Look at you, Tucker," she breathed after finally loosening the hug. She still held his hand.

"Well, look at me," Tucker replied with a smug smile.

"How are you? How was the war?" she asked, almost breathless.

"I survived. Yeah, that's what's most important."

Rosie had tears in her eyes and Tucker told himself he didn't know why. Oh, he knew why. She had a crush on him.

"I'm so glad you're safe, Tucker."

Tucker nodded and looked around the room. "Thanks for staying here while I was away."

"It was a pleasure," Rosie blushed.

He dragged his bag from the door and let it fall on the carpet. "I see you're still packing," he commented.

He noticed the wall had been repainted in pink and orange and his lip jutted out. He shook it off immediately, like it was nothing, and made a mental note to get some reasonable wallpaper. Some wallpaper that wouldn't give him nausea, or just repaint the walls altogether.

"Yes, I'll be done soon and you'll be able to settle in," Rosie replied.

Tucker nodded and sat on his sofa. He missed it. He took off his shoes as he observed Rosie from the top of his eye. She was nervous around him. She liked him, obviously. But no. She just wasn't his type, he told himself. Too farm girly? Ah, he chuckled inside. His descriptions could be cruel. If only Rosie knew what he was thinking about her right then. But she would never know.

He waited as she removed her last box and carried out all the stray cats she had kept in the apartment. After a final hug and some fussing, he dismissed her and smacked his lips when she said she might check on him every now and then.

Rosie, darling, I really don't need anyone to check up on me. Especially not you, Rosie. What, you need a boyfriend? What if I had died at the war? Or never came home? Yeah, right. You'd have found someone else. Find someone else!

Tucker snatched himself from the thoughts that were

already making him look weird to Rosie. "I'll see you around, Rosie. Thank you again," he said.

"You're very welcome, Tucker," she replied, stretching his name.

He closed the door and smacked his lips again. Gosh. What would Officer Rowney say now?

Tucker had little to unpack except for his clothes and shoes. He'd have to buy everything else he needed to get settled in fully, and then he'd have to call his grandfather. He took a cold shower and stayed in for almost an hour. Long showers, relaxing evenings, laughing with friends. He missed everything. But he knew he'd also miss working on missions. He'd miss the rush and danger of facing the enemy. Firearm training, combat, he'd miss that too. The two separate parts of his life always stood at extreme opposites like bitter friends, and now he had to choose one that he wanted to stick with. Civilian life came with its own perks, a lot of perks actually. All you had to do was live. But in the army, you couldn't just live, you had to be responsible for others. He'd wanted to be responsible for others too, but something like his own family, people he cherished.

His phone blared as he stepped out of the bathroom. He rolled his eyes at the noise and picked it up.

"Hey man," he answered.

"Hey Tucker. You still coming over?"

"You never give up, do you? Yeah, I'm coming over."

"That's good. See ya."

Tucker flung the phone across his bed. On their flight back home, Pozo had asked Tucker over and he had promised to come. Like Tucker, Pozo didn't have many family members except his grandparents. He and Pozo met at his first military boot camp and stuck fast to each other. Pozo always joked that they stuck because they were both loners and loners had to stick together.

"I'm not a loner, Pozo. I have friends, girls like me, unlike you," Tucker always protested.

"Really? Show me a girl then." Pozo would chuckle.

Pozo had stuck with him, and Tucker decided he'll do the same for him, any day.

Pozo's grandparents expressed their delight at having Tucker over. The table had a lavish spread and Grandma Kitty urged Tucker and Pozo to eat so they could get the proper nutrition.

"You must reward your body for staying healthy during the war," she said between mouthfuls.

"My body had no choice, Grandma," Pozo said.

Tucker shot him a glance.

"What? What?" Pozo smirked.

"He fell ill at the camp, Grandma Kitty," Tucker said.

The elderly woman gasped.

"Twice."

"So much for his body not having a choice," Grandpa Ronald said.

"Thanks, Gramps," Tucker said gratefully.

Pozo looked at Tucker and signaled, "I'll kill you," with his hand.

Everyone focused on their food, and Grandma Kitty continued her nutrition lecture.

After dinner, Tucker walked with Pozo to Grandpa Ronald's greenhouse farm. The old man was trying out a crossbreed between pineapple and mango. The tree was in the early stages of development, and Grandpa Ronald said he had to look after it every day.

"The nurturing is quite easy. Just don't let them weeds grow," he told Tucker.

"Is this going to be safe to eat?" Tucker asked.

"I bet it will, but we'll see," Grandpa Ronald cackled.

Tucker sensed the uncertainty. It reminded him of how he felt when they had a battle strategy he wasn't sure about, and Declan would hardly listen to any other view apart from his own. Tucker swallowed hard at all he had been through and survived.

"You're awfully pensive," Pozo said.

Tucker's breathing became heavy.

Grandpa Ronald fixed his eyes on him.

Tucker felt uncomfortable under the stares. "Oh no, I was just thinking about something real quick," he explained, stuttering a little.

Grandpa Ronald put a hand on his shoulder. "You're always welcome here, son."

Tucker nodded gratefully and took the old man's hands. "Thank you, Gramps," he said.

Back in the house, Pozo's grandmother was brewing some tea. They had some before Tucker asked Pozo to walk with him.

"What's wrong, man?" Pozo asked when they were alone.

Tucker gently shook his head. "I don't know, Pozo. I feel a little overwhelmed. I don't know what I'm gonna do next and I have a lot I wanna do."

"That makes two of us, bro," Pozo said.

"You're so useless. Thought you were gonna help me figure out my thoughts."

Pozo burst into laughter. Tucker was used to it, Pozo playing about everything. But some humor was always refreshing.

"We're both useless, man. We can't help each other." Pozo cackled.

"Seriously, man." Tucker knew the words he had to say to get Pozo to stop his jokes.

"What? We'll figure it out. I say we relax and goof around a little before we start thinking about those things again."

Tucker nodded in agreement. That was what he needed, to just take things slow.

When they parted, he went to the grocery store to buy some things he needed. He returned home just before eight o'clock that night, and once he had dumped the groceries on the kitchen table, he went to bed and drifted into a deep sleep. He was home.

CHAPTER
FOUR

Something wet was on Tucker's face, nudging him from a dreamless sleep. He turned in the bed, but still the wetness remained. He shook his head and the wet sensation stopped. Tucker jerked awake. He opened an eye and immediately used his palm to shield his eyes from the glare of the morning sun. He looked around for the cause of the wetness, and then he saw it.

The blue and green eyes stared at him, unblinking. Tucker stared back, unblinking. Man and animal continued their stare down till the cat meowed pitifully.

Tucker shook his head. "Just what do you think you're doing? And how did you get in here?" he said.

The cat merely meowed again.

"What? That's supposed to be an answer?"

The cat swished its tail and leapt off Tucker's bed. Tucker watched the animal walk out of the bedroom and shook his head. Stretching, he checked his wall clock and whistled under his breath. Twelve hours. He'd been sleeping for twelve hours. He wondered what Pozo would think of that.

The cat meowed again.

How did the feline get inside his apartment, he wondered

as he got up from his bed and glanced around the room. The apartment was the only thing he had from his life before the army. He wondered why.

Neither willing to find the answer nor go down the resulting train of thought it would conjure, Tucker walked, half-dressed, to the living room and grabbed a small bag. He rummaged inside the bag for his shaving stick and found it.

The cat meowed again.

"Yeah, I know I'm half-naked, so shut it. At least I didn't break into another person's house."

The cat tilted its head to the left, blinked, and started cleaning itself. Tucker narrowed his eyes.

"Oh, so self-righteous, aren't you?"

Meow.

"Well, that's entirely your problem. Just stay out of my room. Don't want your self-righteous cat body on my bed."

The cat purred, fixing on Tucker with a glare that seemed to say, "What bed? The one infested with bugs? That bed?"

"My bed doesn't have bedbugs. And if it did, you brought them!" Tucker retorted, then laughed at himself. He was arguing with what was most likely a stray cat, and he was half-dressed with a shaving stick for a weapon. How the mighty have fallen, he concluded, chuckling as he walked back into the room.

After a relaxing bath, he flopped back onto his bed, heaving a tremendous sigh. He didn't know what to do next. Sure, Pozo's grandparents had invited him over for lunch, but no matter how much he liked Pozo, there was no way he could sit through another one of Pozo's ramblings about war and death, which seemed to excite his grandparents for some reason.

In that moment, Tucker realized he had not called his own grandfather to let him know he was back in town. If the old man found out he was around, he would hound him till he went to visit him.

The answering machine picked up and asked Tucker to leave a message.

"Hey Pops, it's me, Clay. I just got back yesterday, and I'm fine. I'll call you later when I've settled in. Bye."

Tucker clicked off and placed the receiver down. He snatched a pair of worn shorts from an open bag and slipped them on. He heard a crash in the living room and went to inspect the cause.

"You crazy cat. What are you doing?" he hollered, bewildered by the sight that confronted him. The stray was busy attacking a table decoration that looked suspiciously like a rat. Rosie must have left the decoration behind, Tucker surmised. Proceeding with caution, he started moving towards the cat, then was stopped in his tracks by a strident 'niaowrr' from the feline. The cat fixed on him with a glare, and the decoration in its grip.

"That's not food, you furball."

The cat merely looked at him and sat down, switching its attention back to the decoration. The cat pawed the rat, growling softly at it.

Tucker shrugged and left the feline to amuse itself. "Don't break anything," he warned and walked back to the room. He looked at the wall clock. Twenty-five past eight. He had to get some food in his stomach. He decided and hoped cereal would calm the raging storm in his stomach as he walked back to the living room.

The cat barreled at him the moment he entered the room, and Tucker watched the animal as though it was in slow motion, eyes narrowed. The cat launched itself at his ankles and let out a stridulous 'niaowrr'.

"Crazy cat," Tucker muttered before walking to the kitchen.

The cat repeated the action as Tucker removed some cereal from the cabinet, and also when Tucker removed some milk from the fridge. He turned and faced the cat, annoyed.

"What's with you, cat? What do you want from me? You're lucky I haven't thrown you out, but you're pushing your luck."

The cat sat and meowed softly, its eyes following the movement of Tucker's hand as he made himself breakfast. Tucker finally got it.

"Oh, you want some food, is that it?"

The cat merely purred softly.

"Why couldn't you ask nicely, then? Was attacking me really necessary?" he asked, laughing a bit. He glanced around for an empty bowl, and when he found one on the kitchen counter, he poured in some milk and placed it in front of the cat, having a weird feeling of satisfaction as the cat bent to lap the milk. The feline was done and purring for more in less than a minute.

"Greedy, aren't you?" Tucker said, smiling as he bent to pour more milk. He hit his head against the kitchen counter when he stood. "Ouch!" he grunted and was about to blame the cat when he heard the phone ring in his room. He glared at the cat as he left the kitchen.

"Tucker here."

"Now, what do I call myself?" Tucker broke into a smile as he heard the voice. He would recognize the voice anywhere.

"Hi Pops."

"Clarence, how are you?"

"Well, I'm now ex-military," he said.

His grandfather laughed.

"I know. I asked you how you are."

"Well, I'm good. I just got back yesterday, and I miss it already. It's hard to explain."

"I have a feeling it'd be easier to explain if you explain it to me at the cottage."

Tucker chuckled. "Pops."

"What? It was only an innocent suggestion."

Tucker laughed. "There isn't an innocent bone in your body."

"You don't get away with insulting me, young man."

Oh, two can definitely play at this game, Tucker thought affably. "You don't get away with manipulating me, old man," Tucker retorted in a perfect mimic of his grandfather's tone.

His grandfather laughed. "You military brat. Oh, ex-military brat."

Tucker chuckled again. "Low blow, Pops."

"That's what you get for insulting an older man. So, when will you be coming to Madro?"

"You old steamroller," Tucker said before laughing. "Alright, I'll call you soon about the time."

"Good." His grandfather sounded satisfied.

"I missed you, Pops," Tucker confessed gently.

"I know, son. Welcome home."

"Thanks Pops. I guess I'll be seeing you soon."

"Absolutely," his grandfather said.

Tucker grinned. "Don't count on it."

"You've never been any good at lying, Clarence," his grandfather said.

Pops was the only one who never called him Clay. It was always Clarence, every time. It made Tucker smile.

"Bye Pops," he said before clicking off. Happier than he'd been in a long time, Tucker wolfed down the rest of his breakfast and glanced around the apartment.

For the first time in nearly a decade, he had nothing to do in the morning. It was too late to go for a jog, and he wasn't even interested in one at the moment anyway, but was just so used to it.

His cell phone chimed. He picked it up and read the text. He smiled and dialed the number.

"Hey Tucker."

"Jake. You still sound like a college grad in love," Tucker said with a chuckle.

"That's senior accountant to you, Clay," Jake Rowney, Tucker's best and oldest friend, retorted.

"Oh, yeah?"

"Yep. Got the promotion two months ago."

"Congrats man."

"Thanks. Welcome home, bro. Finally I can stop biting my nails and upsetting the wife whenever I hear of our military battling it out with some insurgents or terrorists in the middle of who knows where."

Tucker laughed. "Well, that's the job."

Jake grunted in agreement. "Um, are you okay, man?" he asked.

"What?"

"Well, you know, I'm always hearing about ex-military guys having mental issues and nightmares because of the wars and bloodshed and stuff."

"Oh. Well, I didn't have nightmares last night, and I'm pretty sure I won't tonight either. And as for the mental issues, I don't think I have any. They stationed me in an area where we had to fight off insurgents, nothing mentally disturbing," Tucker said.

"You sure, man?"

"Absolutely."

"Alright," Jake replied, then his voice brightened. "When will you be visiting?"

"What is it with civilians and visiting?"

"Hey, you're a civilian now pal, so watch it."

"Ex-military."

"Still civilian."

Tucker grinned. "Whatever. How's the wife and the runt?"

"My kid's no runt," Jake said.

Tucker laughed. "Yeah, yeah, yeah."

"Well, Rebecca is as great as ever. Also as pregnant as an elephant."

"I'm telling!" Tucker said before ending the call and roaring with laughter.

The phone rang a few seconds later.

"Hello, who is this?" Tucker said before laughing.

"Clay, one word, and I'll have you kidnapped," Jake threatened.

Tucker chuckled. "I'd like to see you try, pretty boy."

"Dude, I'll do anything. Just don't tell her I said that."

"Hmmm," Tucker pretended to think. "Anything?" he asked, laughing.

"Anything man. I'm desperate here."

"Okay. I want a three years' free membership at your gym."

"Get lost. One month and not a day more."

"Then it means I'll tell Rebecca at the end of that month how her sweet husband called her an elephant."

"I didn't! I said she was as pregnant as one!"

"I don't think she's going to be bothering with the metaphor, Jake."

"You evil man!" Jake spluttered.

"Unfortunately, evil men have a lot of control in this world, pal," Tucker said.

"Okay, two months and not a second more."

Tucker grinned wolfishly at the phone. Let the bargaining begin. "Two and a half years."

"Eighteen months."

"Twenty."

"Six months."

"Watch your step, civilian man. Fifteen."

"Twelve."

"Fifteen."

"Either you take twelve or I never speak to you again," Jake said mournfully.

Tucker laughed, enjoying himself. "Alright, twelve months. Free subscription, Jake. I'm not paying for anything."

"Fine. You're a leach, you know."

"Well, this leach is gonna be sucking off a year of free gym membership. Pretty good leaching if you ask me."

"Shut up and don't come to my house. You're not invited."

"I'd love to hear what Rebecca would say if she knew you were the one who stopped her son from seeing his godfather."

Jake burst into laughter at that. "Clay, you're crazy. Really. I've missed you, man. Welcome back, soldier."

"Thanks. But I still want that free gym membership."

"Just don't mention it anywhere around Rebecca."

"Done. When is Rebecca due?"

"Six weeks from now, I think. You know, having one child doesn't make having your second child any less scary."

"Well, you're talking to the most unqualified person for being a father. But one thing I do know is you're a great dad. Nothing can take that away, and that's all you need to remember."

Jake's breathing trembled. "And you said you're unqualified to be a father," he said.

"Yep."

"Well, when are you visiting?"

Tucker grunted.

Jake laughed at his friend.

"Don't hound me, pal," Tucker said.

"When are you coming? Mom would love to see you."

Tucker closed his eyes. He'd missed Mrs. Rowney. "Alright. I'll come to the house today."

"Great. I'll call Mom and—"

"No, Jake. I want to surprise her. I didn't tell her when I was leaving, so I think it'd be right to surprise her."

There was a pause from the other end of the call. "Hmm, that's some weird logic, Clay."

"Just leave it be and don't tell her anything. I feel guilty about leaving for nearly a decade without saying goodbye."

"Alright," Jake relented. "What time will you be coming over?"

"Evening most likely. I have some painting and rearranging to do."

Jake chuckled. "Still staying in that ratty old cage?"

Tucker narrowed his eyes. "Civilian, watch your mouth."

Jake laughed into the phone. "Ex-military, what are you going to do about it?"

"You're a spoilt brat, you know," Tucker said.

"Maybe. But at least I haven't lived in a ratty old cage since college. Get a home man, you're loaded."

"Bye Jake," Tucker said and ended the call. He was going to get back at Jake, he promised, and made a mental note of the promise.

Tucker walked into the living room and glanced around, hands on his hips. His walls had to be repainted, and he had to get some furniture in, he thought. No matter what Jake said, he was comfortable in this apartment, and he wasn't going to get himself some overpriced house that would only increase his expenses and make him look good to people that didn't care about him.

"Hey cat, what color do you think would be great for my walls? I've had them black before, but I want suggestions. Anything?" he asked, fixing his gaze on the brown cat who seemed unconcerned.

"Oh, now that you're full, you couldn't care less. Ungrateful feline."

The cat tilted its head to stare at him, then stood up and walked to him, rubbing its body against his legs.

Tucker was unconvinced.

"Pal, you're not gonna fool me. All you care about is food.

My food." Then he bent down and picked up the cat, stroking its head down to its back.

The cat purred.

Tucker shook his head and walked into his room. He placed the cat gently inside an empty carton beside his bed and started arranging his room. The harsh, high-pitched sound of his phone's ringtone broke his concentration.

"Tucker here."

"Hey Clay, it's Rebecca. Jake just called and said you were back."

"Loudmouth," Tucker said under his breath. "Yeah, lovely. Just got back yesterday."

"That's great. Why didn't you call before you arrived, though? Mom and I would've loved to have picked you up from the airport."

"I'm sorry, Becca."

Rebecca's laugh was quick and delightful. "No, it's not a big deal. So, Jake said you'd be coming over today."

Tucker knew it wasn't a question, but a statement of confirmation. "Yeah. Just don't tell Mrs. Row... Mom. Just don't tell Mom I'm coming over."

"Oh, okay. Why?"

"I'll explain later. Just don't tell her, alright?"

"Alright."

"Thanks. See you later," he said and clicked off.

He flopped onto his bed, face down, wondering what Mrs. Rowney thought of him. He knew what he thought of himself. Turning over, he stared at the ceiling, hands behind his head. The cat suddenly leapt onto the bed, startling him a bit.

"Hey pal."

The feline walked majestically over his body, coming to rest on his chest. Tucker looked at it.

"You know, I don't know why I haven't thrown you out. You're basically a stray cat who could have rabies or any other disease you cats have. Plus, you have bad manners and you only like me for my food, and you won't contribute a dime to the rent. So, pal, how exactly are you useful to me?"

The cat raised its head, meowed softly, then placed its head back down, its green eye open, and stared at Tucker.

Tucker chuckled. "Okay, okay, you're useful as an emotional support cat, even though your ability to empathize is pretty lousy. By the way, I think I'll name you Dunk," he said while gathering his thoughts. "Also, I haven't thrown you out because you remind me of me. Officer Rowney rescued me as a stray just like you are, and he took me in and made me into a man. And how did I repay him? By going to a stupid narcotics deal that cost him his life."

Tucker knew he wasn't supposed to think about it, but he couldn't help himself. He'd woken up feeling subdued that morning, and the weather had echoed his emotions. Maybe if he had taken it as a sign, Officer Rowney would still be alive. It was supposed to be his last petty coke deal before the Badgers left him alone, but it went south pretty fast when he realized they'd set him up. Officer Rowney was in the area on patrol, and when he heard gunshots, he charged in. Tucker remembered the shock on officer Rowney's face when he saw Tucker in the vicinity. It was the same look the officer made when he got shot. The pain and agony that was etched on his face remained seared in Tucker's memory, and he would always relive that moment. Officer Rowney died from his wounds the day after, and Tucker fled the only home he'd ever known because of the guilt. And now he's supposed to go back and face the man's wife, when he's the one responsible for her husband's death.

Distressed, Tucker gently placed the cat down on the bed and walked into the living room. His breathing became labored and he frowned. He squeezed his eyes shut and scrubbed his hands over his face. How was he going to face Mrs. Rowney? He doubted she would even want to see him, and he fully expected her to claw his eyes out the moment she laid eyes on him. He pinched the bridge of his nose, his eyes still shut as he breathed in deeply. Nothing else mattered now, as far as he was concerned. He had to get to the Rowneys' and see Mrs. Rowney. Even if she rejected him, he would know he tried, and he would take his punishment. Tucker walked back to his room and changed his clothes. When he was done, he turned to face the cat.

"Hey, don't eat anything while I'm gone. And stay out of my clothes." Tucker stepped out of the building and hailed a cab.

The cabbie was a rotund, who looked like she could stare down any Special Forces soldier. "Where to?" she asked.

"Lowton's street. There's a gym on the right, about ten blocks from the cinema."

The woman looked at him in the mirror. "Alright. Strap in and prepare for the ride of your life," she said before smacking on the gum in her mouth.

"Could you slow down?" Tucker said for the umpteenth time, as the cabbie wove in between traffic at illegal speeds.

"Whatchu scared of? The cops?"

Tucker narrowed his eyes and sighed. "Slow down!" he said with a healthy dose of authority.

The cabbie complied, but not without grumbling. They arrived at the Rowney's residence about fifteen minutes later.

"Your car's gonna end up in the impound soon if you don't quit driving like a lunatic," Tucker said before stalking off.

The cabbie laughed. "You only live once!"

Tucker shook his head. *Weirdo.*

The walk from the road to the door felt like it took years. Tucker's palm became clammy and his eyes twitched.

Breathing in deeply and rubbing his palms on his pants, he climbed the stairs and knocked on the door.

"Coming," a voice came from the other side.

A moment later, a willow thin lady with curls of fiery red hair opened the door with a smile.

"Hi," she said.

"Hi. I am here to see the Rowneys."

"Of course," she said with a smile. "Rebecca, a very good-looking hunk is here to see your family," she announced in laughter.

Tucker found himself smiling too.

"I'm Miriam, Rebecca's friend. Come in," she said and opened the door wider to let him in.

He stepped in and stared. The house was exactly as he remembered. There were a couple of new art pieces, but those were the only alterations. The gold-colored chandelier still hung from the high ceiling and the dining table sat covered with bowls of food. He glanced at the clock briefly and saw it was around the time the Rowneys normally had lunch. He heard footsteps and looked up. Rebecca was beaming at him, moving as quickly as she could manage with her hands out.

"Clay," she breathed, delighted as Tucker swept her off her feet like the extra weight was nothing.

"You look better every year. I should have waited a little longer. Maybe you'd have chosen me instead of that dork," he said, making her laugh.

"Hey pal, you mind putting my wife down? Just because you're ex-military don't mean you get to steal a man's wife," Jake said as he stepped into the airy living room.

Tucker chuckled and gently dropped Rebecca to her feet.

"Ex-military?" Miriam said, her eyes twinkling.

Tucker nodded.

"Just came home?"

"Obviously, Sherlock," Jake said to her before catching Tucker in a bear hug.

"Oh man, you've got some pouch in your middle," Tucker said.

Everyone laughed, except Jake.

"Hey pal, I can still take you on, so watch your mouth."

"I don't know, Jake. He looks like he would wipe the floor with you," Miriam said.

"Hey!" Jake protested.

"Don't mind them, Jake," Mrs. Rowney said as she stepped off the stairs and into the living room. "You have other talents apart from physicality," she concluded as everyone laughed, except Tucker.

His gaze met with Mrs. Rowney's, and for a few seconds neither said anything.

"Hello Clarence," she said, breaking the brief silence. She held out her arms and smiled at him.

Tucker moved into the embrace, not sure of his feelings.

"Welcome home, son."

Tucker breathed in shakily and held her tighter.

"Excuse us," Mrs. Rowney said to everyone as she led Tucker upstairs.

She opened the door to her room, entered, and sat on the bed. Tucker stared at her.

"Come," she invited with a pat on the bed.

He stepped in and closed the door. "Mrs. Rowney, I'm sorry. I did...."

"Son, there's nothing to be sorry about," she said.

Tucker opened his mouth to speak again.

She shushed him.

"Clarence, welcome home. We've all missed you. Look at you." She smiled at him as she placed her palm on his cheek and stared at his face. "My son has become a man," she said, smiling through wet eyes.

"Mrs. Rowney."

"Judith," she corrected.

"Mom," Tucker said.

Tears fell from Judith's eyes. "I've waited for so long to hear that again."

"I'm sorry I didn't call, Mom. I'm very sorry," Tucker apologized, his eyes blurry with unshed tears.

"It's okay. You're here now. It's okay," she soothed, stroking his hair gently.

"I missed you," he said after a moment. "I missed you so much, but I was afraid to call because I blamed myself. I blamed myself for his death. I blamed myself for coming into your lives, because if I hadn't, you'd still have your husband today. Your family would've been complete, and all that's my fault."

Judith looked at him with knitted eyebrows. "Now where you get off thinking such things? If you hadn't come into our lives, what's to say Henry wouldn't have died in the line of duty anyway? What's to say he wouldn't have died in a car crash, or in a swimming accident? Don't you see, Clarence? It's not your fault he died, not at all," she said in a gentle tone.

"But he died trying to protect me."

"Yes, but that doesn't make it your fault. He did what every good father would do, try to protect his child. His death was the fault of the person who pulled the trigger, understand?"

Tucker nodded solemnly.

"Good. Henry left you something. I'll go get it for you," Judith said before standing.

"Mom," Tucker called, stopping her in her tracks.

"Yeah?"

"I love you," he said.

Judith's eyes filled, and she held out her arms. Tucker walked into her embrace for the second time that day.

"Don't go away anymore," she whispered.

"Okay Mom. I'm here now," he said after releasing her from the hug. "I'm here," he repeated.

Judith nodded and walked to her wardrobe, brought out a

medium-sized box, and placed in on the bed. "Henry said to give you this. He said you'd know the code."

Tucker stared at her. "Code?"

"Yes," she said with a chuckle. "Apparently he didn't trust me not to open the box and read its contents."

Read, Tucker thought. *Why you clever woman.* "Mom," he said, smiling. "You've opened the box, haven't you?"

Her smile was an innocent one. "How could I open a locked box?"

"Really? Then how did you know the contents are to be read?"

Judith laughed richly. "You've always been a smart one."

Tucker grinned and opened the box. He smiled when he saw what was inside.

CHAPTER
FIVE

Tucker went back downstairs ahead of Judith, who wanted to use the restroom.

"You know, Becca," he said as he came down. "I have some dirt on this guy and I can tell you everything right now."

Rebecca giggled and moved stealthily towards Tucker, her stomach protruding.

"Tell me, tell me," she whispered.

Tucker shot a glance at Jake and mouthed, "You're toast."

He whispered into Rebecca's right ear and she frowned. She turned around and looked at Jake, who was already fuming.

"Whatever he said, he's a big fat liar," Jake said.

"He's not even big or fat!" Miriam said. "I mean, have you seen him?"

Jake frowned. "Of course I've seen him. He's my brother."

"Nah, I don't think you've really seen him. If you have, you wouldn't call him big or fat."

Tucker laughed at Jake, and Rebecca joined in.

"Pardon .this accountant person. He's not seen me in

years, and calling me names is his way of whining that he's missed me."

Jake rolled his eyes. "You wish!"

Mrs. Rowney walked downstairs and touched Miriam's shoulder.

"These boys confuse me sometimes. They can't stay together, but can't stay away from each other either."

"No, Mom," Jake said. "He's the one who can't stay away from me."

Rebecca held her husband's cheeks and kissed him. "Stop protesting and focus on me," she said.

"Ew, guys, get a room or something," Miriam said while giggling.

Tucker was going to speak, but changed his mind when Jake silenced him with a raised finger.

Jake pulled his wife in and they kissed deeper.

Judith smiled and winked at Tucker. He smiled back at her, genuinely happy that Jake and Rebecca were happy.

After the couple had released their embrace, Miriam cleared her throat.

"Rebecca, do you need any help getting lunch ready?" she asked.

Tucker saw an opportunity and rose to the occasion. "I'd like to take everyone's order because I'm cooking this afternoon," he announced.

"You can cook too?" Miriam asked, wide-eyed.

Tucker nodded.

Jake beamed proudly. "There's nothing this man can't do," he said.

Tucker waited for the balancing comment, which he was sure would come.

"Except…" Jake started.

Tucker raced behind his friend and covered his mouth, stopping him from saying the next word.

"One more word, senior accountant, and I'll lock you in

the treehouse," Tucker threatened, speaking directly into Jake's ear.

He released his hold on Jake and allowed him to catch his breath. Once his breathing regulated, Jake jumped up and chased Tucker upstairs, growling like a hungry lion.

The women laughed hard and Rebecca sat to rest her legs.

"They don't know they're too old for this," Judith said amidst her laughs.

The stomping of feet started back towards them and the laughter continued.

"Okay," Jake panted.

Tucker was not panting at all.

"I'll let you make lunch so my lovely wife can eat, and because I don't want your playful butt to wake Micah."

Everyone laughed, then Tucker went to the kitchen.

He prepared to work and preheated the large family air fryer. He fried mozzarella sticks, cheese curds and chicken wings. Rebecca helped him serve the family, but he made sure she had as little of the work as possible to do.

Miriam enthused over Tucker's cooking and said she had never tasted chicken wings so well cooked.

"It's my secret recipe," Tucker said softly, knowing it made Miriam's heart melt.

"This chicken is really good, Clay. How did you learn to cook so well?" she asked.

"By cooking a lot. It's a passion I discovered while in the military."

"Oh, that's wonderful, son," Judith said, eyes twinkling.

"You could make a great living from this. It's fantastic," Rebecca said.

Tucker looked at her and laughed.

"No, seriously, Clay. I mean, even I have never tasted chicken so good."

"I agree with Rebecca, totally. This food is great," Jake added.

. . .

After the meal, Tucker and Jake did the dishes and finally had some time alone in the kitchen.

"It's so refreshing to see you, man," Jake said.

Tucker shook his head. This was the time for man talk and he was going to tell Jake how much he missed him too.

"I'm sorry about everything, Jake," Tucker said. "I didn't know what else to do."

Jake placed a dish in the sink and turned to Tucker.

"Clay, I don't blame you for anything."

Tucker nodded. "You miss him?"

Jake pursed his lips and exhaled. "Every day," he said.

"That's my fault, Jake. If it wasn't for me, he'd still be here."

"But nobody knows that for sure," Jake said. "Honestly, bro, I think you should forgive yourself for everything. You miss Dad, I miss Dad, we all miss Dad. But Dad left a great legacy behind. You, Clarence."

Tucker looked directly at Jake, who continued talking.

"Your Dad's legacy. I am too. The day Dad brought you home, I was thrilled. You're the reason I have someone to call my brother."

Tucker clenched his jaw tight. "I still owe you an apology."

Jake took in a deep breath, then exhaled. "If you insist," he said while shaking his head.

Tucker clasped both hands together. "Jake, Dad died because he was trying to save me. I'm sorry about that. He took me in and tried to give me a better life, but I believed the lies of those thugs and took a job. I brought all of this on us, and I'm sorry. I'm sorry, Jake."

Jake was quiet for a few seconds. He took in another breath and exhaled before nodding. "No problem. But I'm not sorry that Dad found you. I'm not sorry he died in honor, saving a child. And I'm not sorry you're my brother."

Tucker embraced him as he finished the last sentence, and both of them groaned at the tightness of the hug.

"You've been a loyal brother, Jake," Tucker said.

"Does that mean you'll quit gossiping about me and stop being such a pain in the butt?"

"Nah," Tucker replied. "You can only wish. I'll never get off your case."

<hr>

Tucker left the Rowneys late that evening after Jake had pestered him hard about finding a woman and settling down. Tucker declined when Jake suggested Miriam. She was a great girl, but he wasn't ready to date anyone just yet. He didn't even have a job or a steady income.

"You're loaded," Jake had protested.

"Why do you keep saying that?" Tucker asked. "You, of all people, know how these numbers work. If you don't make any money, you'll go broke."

"I agree with you, bro," Jake said. "First things first, then."

Tucker was glad he got through to Jake. Dating was not the right thing for him at the time. He had to figure out his life first. Tucker took a cab and gave instructions to the driver, not forgetting to add, "Please drive carefully and don't go too fast."

The drive was smooth, and he was on his street within ten minutes. He paid the cabbie and went into the corner store to buy some chocolates. He picked out his favorite brands of Mars and Snickers and left the store before opening a bar and chewing it as he walked. Tucker missed indulging himself in Snickers. At that thought, he turned a corner and couldn't believe what happened next. He was standing face to face with a boy holding a penknife and asking him to hand over his wallet. The boy came out of nowhere and was fast on his feet.

Tucker raised his hands and stayed still. "Young man, you don't want to do this," he said.

"Pass the wallet before I hurt you!" the boy yelled.

In one fluid movement, Tucker snatched the penknife from the boy and knocked him out cold. Tucker looked carefully at the mugger. A teenager. Fourteen, maybe fifteen. He considered for a few seconds what he should do with him, but knew he couldn't leave him there.

It thoroughly appalled Tucker. Now what? A teenager he'd knocked out cold. He picked up the thin boy, noticing the scratches on his face. He must have been fighting a lot or something. How does a teenager even attempt to steal from an ex-military soldier? Well, the kid didn't know he was ex-military, Tucker reminded himself. But stealing from a man as big as he was, how daring can a teenager be?

From his calculation, the boy either ran away from home or had no home at all. The image of himself as a little boy flashed before his eyes and he grunted under the weight of the teenager. As Tucker approached his apartment, he saw two figures standing a few meters away from his door. It was definitely a woman and a child. Tucker paused momentarily before continuing toward his apartment with a slower stride. He came face to face with the tall woman and immediately noticed tiny dimples cutting into her smooth, almond-colored cheeks. She held the small hand of a boy sporting a low-fade cut while her other hand held a basket of food. The woman let out a frightened gasp when Tucker came under the light and she saw the unconscious teenager on his shoulder.

"What the—" She stepped away from Tucker, pulling the little boy closer to her.

Tucker noticed the resemblance between both of them and figured the little boy was her son.

"Hello?" Tucker raised his brow, expecting an explanation. Although he could guess what this was about, he was not particularly in the mood for some visiting women. He had just knocked out a teenager and needed to take care of him.

"Can I help you?" Tucker asked. *Be nice, Clay, be nice.*

"The boy—" the woman gasped again, pointing at the teenager.

"He's fine. He tried to mug me, so I hit him, and now I have to make sure he's okay," Tucker said.

"Oh," the little boy said.

"Sssshhh," his mother silenced briskly, but said nothing after.

Tucker shifted on his feet and adjusted the teenager on his shoulder.

"What can I do for you?" he asked again, wondering why you had to ask civilians a question about three times before you got an answer.

"I-I'm Catherine. Catherine Landers, and this is my son, Jerry," she said.

Tucker adjusted his stance with impatience.

Catherine noticed. "Oh, um, it was Jerry's idea to bring you some food. We live across the hall from you, there." She pointed in the opposite direction.

Tucker's gaze followed her finger. Then he nodded. "Thank you," he said as his eyes wandered around the hall.

"Please don't mention it. We just wanted to welcome you back to the neighborhood."

Tucker took out his keys and opened the door. "Please come in," he said, going in first.

He turned on the switch and Dunk came out of his box, meowing loudly.

"That's Dunk, don't worry, he's just not used to having so many people around," Tucker said before laying the teenager on the sofa, going to the bathroom, grabbing a towel and soaking it in cold water, and returning to the living room. "Please sit down," he said to Catherine and Jerry.

Catherine found two low chairs and sat with Jerry, who was speaking small words to Dunk.

Tucker sat by the unconscious teenager and wiped his face with the cold towel.

"Is he going to be alright?" Catherine asked.

Tucker noticed in that moment she had a sweet voice. "Yes," he answered without looking back. "He should be waking up soon."

Catherine nodded.

"So, you said you wanted to welcome me back. How did you know I was ever here?" Tucker asked. He finished wiping the teenager's face before turning to the mother and her little son.

"Rosie told me you lived here, and that she was watching the house while you were away."

"I see. Did she tell you where I was?"

"No, she didn't tell me that."

Tucker nodded. Good thing she knows nothing of his past. Although it worried him why he didn't want her to know anything about his past, he found himself satisfied with not saying anything about being in the military.

"We have to go now." Catherine got up from the chair.

Dunk circled her, meowing and holding his tail up. Jerry attempted to touch one of his paws, and Dunk stopped to look at the small hand reaching for him. He meowed again, and Jerry laughed.

"I think he likes me, Mom," he said with excitement.

Tucker smiled.

"Thank you for the food. I've already had dinner, but I'll keep it for when the kid wakes up."

"I like your beard, mister," Jerry said in a whinny voice.

"Oh yeah?" Tucker bent over to level with Jerry. "I'll keep it for you, then."

Catherine laughed nervously, and Tucker patted the boy's hair.

"Thanks for telling Mommy to bring me some food," he said.

"Pleasure. Can I call you Uncle Tuck?"

"Uncle Tuck?" Tucker said with a chuckle. "Yeah, I like it. We have a deal."

Jerry raised his hand for a hi-five and Tucker took it, laughing.

Catherine scooped the boy in her hands and they headed out.

"Thank you, Catherine," Tucker said as he opened the door for them.

"You're welcome, Tucker. Do have a good night."

"You too. Bye, Jerry."

"Bye, Uncle Tuck. See you tomorrow."

Tucker closed the door behind them and turned around in one swift motion. *Interesting.* As if in agreement, Dunk meowed loudly and turned on his back, letting his legs hang in the air for a few seconds.

"What's with you?" Tucker asked.

Dunk sprawled and went quiet.

"You didn't just tell me to keep my mouth shut, did you?"

Dunk meowed.

"Wonderful. You'll have to work for your dinner tonight."

With that, Tucker headed back to his bathroom. A shower was long overdue.

The food smelled great, and even though Tucker already had dinner, he couldn't resist taking a bite from the fish casserole, then eventually the cake.

"Wow," he said. "Good stuff."

The last time he had casserole that tasted so good was more than a decade ago. Officer Rowney took him and Jake on a tour when they were fourteen. It was outside of the city, a great place for a getaway. And although Tucker was young, he knew he'd love to go back to Cups & Bites. They served great casserole and was the most popular restaurant in the area. He wanted to go back there and experience it again. He could never forget the great time and all he'd learned while with Mr. Rowney.

"I miss you so much, man," he muttered, his mood suddenly changing.

Dunk felt the change and meowed towards Tucker.

Tucker looked at the approaching cat and cut a piece of casserole for him. "You'd have loved him, Dunk," he mumbled. "He took care of stray boys like me so I can take care of stray cats like you." Tucker paused. "Officer Rowney was a great man, Dunk. He was my hero, still is. Removed me from the streets and gave me a good life. I wanna be that kinda man."

Tucker looked at the boy on the sofa. Dunk looked at him too.

"That one, he mugged me."

Dunk looked down and meowed quietly.

"What, you're blaming me? I didn't hurt him. He was trying to steal from me."

Dunk looked away.

Tucker frowned at him. Since when could a cat guilt trip him? He stamped his feet on the floor.

Dunk jumped.

"There was nothing I could do, just know that," Tucker said.

Tucker stood from his fight and make-up session with the cat and went to get some milk. "Now, Dunk, even if you refuse to understand and support me, I forgive you and I choose to be nice to you, unlike you." He bit hard into the last two words.

He poured some milk into Dunk's bowl and watched him eat. Tucker looked at the still-fast-asleep teenager and wondered where he came from. The kid looked rough, and Tucker was afraid the young man might be dealing drugs like he did at that age. During the dark days of selling cocaine to young boys and being a middleman for lieutenants who weren't much older than teenagers. The sole of one of the young man's shoes flapped, and he wore faded jeans and a dingy Nike shirt. Tucker restrained himself from being filled with rage toward the parents who had such children and didn't take care of them. He knew when or if he had children of his own, he'd do everything in his power to keep them safe.

Tucker chuckled a little at the thought, his embitterment not leaving him one bit. He carried the boy from the sofa and laid him on the bed. Tucker stood over the still body and hoped the teenager was not yet beyond saving. He left the boy alone in the bed and called Dunk to come help him finish painting.

"Not like you can paint, even if that was all I asked from you for rent," Tucker said to the cat.

Dunk sat down without making a sound while Tucker threw on a nylon apron to keep the paint from staining his clothes. He then turned his speaker on low and worked on his walls. It was such an odd hour to paint a room, but he didn't care.

Tucker had just finished painting the last section of the wall when he heard the boy wake up and walk into the living room.

"Well, well, well," he said, turning to face the teenager.

"How did I get here?" the boy asked.

Tucker raised a brow. *Cocky kid, how nice.*

"You," the boy said. "Who are you?"

Tucker put the paintbrush back in the bucket and took off his apron. "Isn't it obvious?" he snarled. "I'm the man you tried to rob. The man who told you to change your mind, but you held a knife against anyway."

The boy was not budging. "You almost killed me. I'll report you to the police," he said.

Tucker laughed. "Quit it, boy. I hold the cards here. I'm the one who can take you to a juvenile home and have you confined there. I'm the one with a case, not you."

The boy recoiled quickly and fidgeted.

"Oh, don't worry," Tucker said. "I won't do any of that. Do you know why?"

The boy shook his head.

"It's because I once was like you, except I was a better

mugger than you. And my father helped me, gave me another chance."

The teenager scoffed. "You had a father. Congratulations. I have nobody."

Tucker ignored him and continued. "My father, a man with amazing character, found me when I was dealing coke downtown and he took me in, instead of turning me in."

"Well, you were his son. Why would he turn you in?"

"I wasn't his son. He was a total stranger. He became my father after that day when he took me to his home and cared for me."

The boy looked at Tucker.

"Yeah, I know you're surprised. I was too," Tucker said. "He was the best man I ever set my eyes on."

The young man nodded.

"He's the reason I won't turn you in, and you should be grateful."

Tucker left the boy in the living room and went into the bedroom. He needed to regain his composure. He sat on the bed and thought for a while. His eyes rested on the box that Mrs. Rowney had given him as a gift from her husband. His father.

I'll never stop missing you, Dad. And it's more difficult for me now that I'm back home. But I promise I'll be good.

Tucker stood and returned to the living room to find the boy sitting on the sofa. He was very still.

"What's your name?" Tucker asked.

"Dwayne," he quietly said.

"Mm? Nice name. I'm Clarence, Clarence Tucker. You can call me Clay or Tucker or Tuck or whatever."

"Thank you," Dwayne said, quietly again.

Tucker said nothing. He waited for some more words.

"I'm sorry, I was hungry and… I was hungry and scared and…"

Tucker remained quiet.

"The group said I had to do it to become a true member of their gang. They said I'd suffer in the streets without them, and I'd be nothing without them…"

The room went silent.

Tucker stood by the kitchen counter. He could see that Dwayne had delicate features, a face that begged for some love. Tucker could also see that he had a lot of fear inside him.

"Dwayne," Tucker called.

Dwayne looked up and his right eyebrow twitched delicately.

"You and only you are responsible for the choices you make in your life."

Dwayne pressed his lips together. "I think my parents decided that for me."

"They decided the past. Only you can decide your future."

Dwayne stared, his lips still pressed.

"Hungry?" Tucker asked.

Dwayne nodded.

He put the fish casserole on a plate and asked Dwayne to help himself with some juice from the table top fridge.

"This food was brought by some good neighbors who admire you," Tucker said.

Dwayne's eyes popped. "Me?"

"Of course not, dummy. I was talking about myself," Tucker said, stone-faced.

Dwayne's nose wrinkled, and he took the plate from Tucker, who allowed him to eat his food while he cleaned up and put away the paint supplies. Tucker felt a surge of hope in him. Maybe the boy was redeemable after all. But the big picture made little sense to him. How is it that life was repeating itself to him? He could see his fifteen-year-old self in Dwayne. He was supposed to be mad at him, but he found himself pitying the teenager, and he knew that wasn't normal. Tucker was a die-hard dealer in facts and logic who believed that everything was a product of choice. But what choice did he have as a kid? And Dwayne? What choice did Dwayne have to be born or not to be born?

"I guess there are choices people will make for you in this world then," Tucker muttered.

He returned to find Dwayne finished with his food and downing the juice.

"He—ey," Tucker calmed him. "Are you still hungry?"

Dwayne nodded.

Tucker gave him some of the cake that Catherine brought, and Dwayne dug in, without taking a breath.

"That bad, huh?" Tucker chuckled.

Dwayne grunted, and his breathing intensified.

"Slow down, pal," Tucker cautioned him.

Tucker sat down and watched Dwayne finish his food. He stayed with the young man to make sure he didn't choke on the food.

"Easy, kid," Tucker cautioned again.

Dwayne breathed. "Thank you," he muttered as he picked up the last crumbs of cake from his plate.

Tucker poured him more juice, and Dwayne drank it all in one gulp.

Tucker's eyes widened, and his mouth gaped. "Whoa!" He had never seen a young person eat so fast.

"The only thing I've had in the past two days was a soda," Dwayne explained.

Tucker nodded. The familiar feeling of intense hunger refreshed in his memory.

"And I stole the soda," Dwayne continued. "I don't want to go to a foster home."

"And why's that?" Tucker asked.

"I learned my father was raised in a foster home. He still turned out to be a bad person."

"Bad person?"

"He hit me a lot," Dwayne said.

Tucker's chest heaved, and he released a long slow exhale, but said nothing.

"He's dead now."

"I'm sorry," Tucker said.

"My mom's dead too. She had cancer."

Tucker stood still, listening to the familiar story.

"I have an aunt who was gonna take me in, but I refused to go with her."

"May I ask why?"

"She was going to molest me."

Tucker hung his head and shook it.

"Yeah, I ran from her. And been in the streets ever since."

Tucker gave Dwayne a chance to breathe and an opportunity for the teenager to decide if he was going to cry or not. The young man held back his tears.

"What are you gonna do now, Dwayne?" Tucker asked in a gentle tone. He knew that no matter how much he cared about the teenager, he had to let him make his own choices.

Dwayne shrugged. "Keep surviving, I guess."

Tucker drew a chair and sat in front of him.

"That's not good enough. What's the plan?"

"People like me don't have a plan. We just wing it."

Tucker smiled. The kid reminded him of himself so much. He decided not to push the issue and to give the kid time to figure things out.

"You know, my dad and I used to live in a trailer downtown. I never met my mom. I don't even know if she's alive," Tucker said.

"Did you mug adults too?" Dwayne asked.

"Many times. I stole from shops too. The darkest of all was selling drugs to other kids."

"Did you use drugs yourself?"

Tucker shook his head. "No, just served as the middleman for pushing the stuff. I hated alcohol and drugs, still do."

"Why?"

"My father was an alcoholic. He drank so much he didn't know what he was doing sometimes."

"Did he hit you?"

Tucker nodded briefly and looked away. "He was just never there and didn't care how I got fed or lived. He left for work one day and returned crying. I tried to help him and he pushed me away."

"What happened after?"

"He jumped from the top of a building some days later, and that was it."

Dwayne was on the edge of his seat.

"So, I never had any real relationship with my parents."

"I'm sorry, Tucker."

Tucker looked up. "Don't be sorry for me, Dwayne. I've done well for myself. But you—"

"I'm just a teenager. There's no one to help me."

"No? Then help yourself, would you? Because in a few years from now, no one will care what happened to your mom or dad. All they'd want to know is how you've built yourself."

Tucker kept his gaze on Dwayne as he spoke to ensure he was getting through to the boy.

Dwayne shook his head as he appeared to ponder over what Tucker had said.

While Tucker waited for the young man's response, he went to the kitchen and poured himself a glass of juice.

Dwayne stood from his chair. And as he did, Tucker again realized how thin the boy was.

"What am I going to do? If I don't do what I do, I'd go hungry, I'll starve, and the kids will hate me."

"The kids on the street are not your friends, Dwayne. They're a bunch of confused fellows just like you."

"But they're kids with terrible parents, like me."

"That doesn't mean you should stick with them, pal," Tucker said.

He chose his words carefully. He didn't want to give Dwayne too much to handle, but he wouldn't stand for him spitting out nonsense either.

Dwayne sat down again.

Tucker poured another glass of juice for him and this time, the boy sipped gently. He was relaxing, which was a good thing.

"What am I gonna do?"

"You tell me," Tucker threw the question back at Dwayne. He was aching to decide for him, to tell him he had to leave his past behind and go to school. He was aching to tell the kid that he was willing to help him, but Dwayne had to decide if he really wanted that.

Tucker's phone rang, and he correctly guessed the caller. He gestured to Dwayne that he was taking the call.

"Hey, man," he spoke into the receiver.

"Clay, I guess you got home safe?" Jake asked.

"Thankfully, I did," Tucker said while eyeing Dwayne.

"Rebecca says hi and we hope to see you more often."

"Tell Becca to make a list of everything she'd want me to cook for her, and it's done."

"What?" Jake breathed. "You want her to get fatter than now? Like a big fat elephant?"

"You know you just give me more dirt to throw on you, right?"

"You're my best friend. You wouldn't dare."

Tucker laughed. "Thanks for having me, man."

"Good night, bro."

Jake clicked off.

Dwayne was assuming. "Girlfriend?"

Tucker crinkled his nose and felt like punching Dwayne's.

"Did you hear me say thanks for having me, man? Or you're just being dangerously deaf?"

Dwayne considered for a while. "I think it's the second one."

Tucker scoffed with a small frown. He checked the time. 10:36 pm.

"So, tell me what you wanna do," Tucker said, getting back to the question at hand.

Dwayne hesitated. "I know I want to try. I mean, these streets are too dangerous. Plus, I don't like going days with little to no food, and I always have to look over my shoulder."

Tucker allowed him to continue speaking.

"Some time ago, I stole from a man and he chased me. I nearly died. But I don't have anywhere to go to."

"We'll get there," Tucker said. "Tell me exactly what you want."

"A good life, I guess. I want a family. I want to go to school."

"You want to go to school?" Tucker asked.

"Yes, or do you think I can't go to school anymore?"

"You can, pal. And you can shine too."

Dwayne nodded, his eyes brightened, and a small smile arched on his face.

Tucker could see hope filling the young man. "You know, Officer Rowney found me stealing from a shop and, rather than turn me in, he took me home. I wasn't knocked out the way you were, but I didn't attack him either."

Dwayne looked down.

"That wasn't meant to make you feel bad. I'm just telling you what happened."

Dwayne nodded.

"His family welcomed me and I became one of them. His son is my best friend now."

"Nice," Dwayne said. "Where's Officer Rowney now?"

Tucker bit his lower lip and held it in. "He died."

Dwayne imitated Tucker's biting of the lip, trying to feel his pain.

"He lives on inside of me. And that's why I'd like to offer you a home here. If you want, you can live with me."

Dwayne shook his head. "I'm a terrible kid. Nobody wants me around them."

"I'll let you believe whatever you decide, Dwayne. But you're welcome to stay."

Dwayne looked up at him and held his gaze. "I'll come here sometimes," he said.

"As you wish, Dwayne. But you better not get in any trouble."

"Thank you."

Tucker stood and stretched.

"I'll leave in the morning," Dwayne said.

Tucker nodded.

"What did you do after Officer Rowney died?"

"I joined the military."

Dwayne's eyes widened. "I knew it! You took my knife too easily."

"Yeah, and I threw away the knife too."

Dwayne was quiet for a moment. "Actually, I'll need that knife. The street is too dangerous not to hold a weapon," he finally said.

"Whatever you do, Dwayne, don't go back to the streets."

"Not even to say goodbye?"

"Goodbye to who?" Tucker raised his voice and Dwayne stiffened.

"Nobody will let you leave them for a better life without trying to hinder you," Tucker said.

"My friends…"

"You have no friend there, Dwayne. The sooner you get it, the better."

Dwayne's chest heaved and Tucker left him alone again. He went to the bathroom and fumed while he brushed his teeth. He was desperately trying to get Dwayne to avoid making the same mistakes that he made. The wild life didn't allow a person to have a clear view of who one's friend or enemy was. It was all a jungle, not right for kids or adults, for that matter. He finished brushing his teeth and went back to meet Dwayne, who was lying down on the couch.

"Ready to go to sleep, pal?" Tucker asked.

"Yeah," Dwayne said softly.

Tucker nodded and got an old duvet from his box. He added a pillow and gave them to Dwayne.

"Thanks," Dwayne said.

"Sleep tight."

"You too."

Tucker turned off the lights and went into the bedroom. After taking off his clothes, he checked on Dunk, who was still asleep in his box. Tucker lay with his back down and, as he stared at the ceiling, he pondered over how things had happened so fast. He breathed gently to calm himself. Even though he wasn't sure if he was doing the right thing for Dwayne, he decided to sleep on it. *Everything will become clear by morning,* he hoped as he closed his eyes. It had to be, because if it wasn't, he didn't have a clue what to do from there.

CHAPTER
SEVEN

Early the next day, Dwayne left the apartment. He didn't give a reason other than he needed to clear his head. Distracted by the cat's persistent meows, Tucker glanced up from his sketch pad, feeling irritated and wondering if Dwayne would return.

"Dunk, no more eating. You've finished an entire jar of milk. What's wrong with you?"

The cat, used to Tucker's blaming and recriminations, merely twitched its tail and continued lapping its milk.

A knock sounded at the door.

"Dunk, get the door," Tucker said absentmindedly as he continued his sketching.

"How's a cat supposed to open the door, soldier?" Dwayne said as he stepped inside.

Tucker smiled. "The prodigal son returns," he said with his head still bowed and his hands still dancing furiously on his sketch pad.

"Hey," Dwayne began as he sank into the old sofa. "I told you I'd come back, didn't I?"

Tucker merely grunted. Dwayne shrugged and turned on the TV. A few minutes after, Tucker looked up and saw the young man completely engrossed in a reality show. For the life of him, Tucker couldn't understand why people wasted their time with such shows and wondered if Dwayne had eaten. He also wondered where he had gone all day, but he decided not to press the boy. They presently had something of a truce, but Tucker still wasn't sure if the boy would stay or go. He wished he would stay, though he'd never come out and admit it. But he knew from experience that no matter what he wished, Dwayne would do whatever he thought was best for himself. All Tucker could do was try his best to put the teenager on the right path.

"Dwayne," Tucker called.

No answer.

"Dwayne."

Again, no answer. Tucker switched off the TV with the remote.

"Hey!" Dwayne protested.

"It got your attention, didn't it?"

Dwayne frowned. "What do you want?"

"Have you eaten today?"

"What's it to you?"

"Don't get snappy with me, young man."

Dwayne narrowed his eyes. "No."

"No, you haven't eaten, or no, you'll get snappy with me?"

"No, I haven't eaten."

"Good. See, wasn't so hard now, was it?"

"Can I go back to the show now?"

Tucker nodded. "Yeah, I guess you can. Or you can come with me and get something to eat," he said. "I'll be ready to go after I use the bathroom."

When Tucker returned from the bathroom, he saw Dwayne patting Dunk's head. He shrugged at the two and continued toward the door.

"Dunk, how do you live with this, dude?" Dwayne asked

the cat as he abandoned the reality show and followed Tucker out the door.

"What's your order, sir?" the waitress, a tiny woman with a broad smile, asked Dwayne.

"Do you—" Tucker started.

"I'll have a hamburger, a coke, some chocolate cake and an apple," Dwayne interrupted before smiling.

"Excellent choices," the waitress said while smiling at Dwayne.

When the waitress left, Tucker looked at Dwayne.

"What?"

Tucker shook his head and smiled.

"That's weird, man."

Tucker glanced at him. "What is?"

"The entire thing with you shaking your head and the smile. In fact, this entire night is weird. First, you take me to a fancy restaurant like I'm your girl, then you're surprised when I order something for myself, and then you smile like some great king who's amused with his slave's choices."

The kid has a rant in him, Tucker chuckled. "Slave? I never knew you were my slave."

"I'm not your slave!"

"Exactly what I was thinking."

Dwayne narrowed his eyes at Tucker. "Because you're ex-military, you think you're better than me? Or is it because you're older?"

Where was this coming from? Tucker wondered. "Er, I don't think we are talking about the same thing anymore, Jake," Tucker said, the name error intentional.

"My name is Dwayne!" he said through clenched teeth.

"Oh, your son has a nice name, sir," the waitress said, smiling as she put their orders on the table.

Tucker knew Dwayne was about to correct her. "Not a word, young man. Or I'll ground you," Tucker said.

Dwayne waited until the waitress left before launching into another tirade. "Son? You're not my dad, and you'll never be. What…"

"I suggest you eat your food, Dwayne. I'm just messing with you."

Dwayne glanced at him before biting into his hamburger. Tucker grinned. They were definitely getting somewhere.

The walk home was quiet, both of them left to their own thoughts. Tucker deliberated on what time would be best to visit his grandfather. Heck, what was he thinking? *The right time to visit Grandpa Mark?* He chuckled softly. He decided he'd go the next day. It was long overdue, and if he was being honest with himself, he had really missed seeing his grandfather.

"Dwayne."

"Yeah."

"I'm traveling tomorrow."

The expression on Dwayne's face suggested he wanted to ask where to and when Tucker would be back. "Okay," was all he said instead.

"Will you stay at the apartment while I'm gone? I need someone to watch Dunk for me."

Dwayne's eyes lit up like a kid locked in a chocolate store. "It'll cost you."

Tucker laughed, genuinely amused. "How much?"

"Twelve bucks an hour."

"For that price, I'll just get professional help that won't eat my food, watch my TV, or sleep in my house."

"That's mean," Dwayne said.

Tucker was about to respond, but saw a figure melt into the shadows a block away.

"Stop," he ordered Dwayne.

"I saw him too."

"How do you know it's a male?"

"He's my friend."

Tucker stopped in his tracks and turned to Dwayne so that the two faced each other.

"He's your friend? You're friends with a mugger?"

"It's not rocket science. I was a mugger," Dwayne said with a shrug, as if he completely explained himself.

"Listen carefully. You are to cease all contact with him and every other mugger, understand? No contact, none."

"No." The single word was laden with defiance.

"You think being a mugger is cool? Ripping people off? Endangering their lives?"

"You think being homeless is cool? Having no one who cares? Not knowing where you're gonna sleep at night?" Dwayne said, before walking ahead.

Tucker watched Dwayne give the person some money and walk off. He was relieved when he saw the teenager walking back toward the apartment building. When Tucker arrived home five minutes later, he saw Dwayne glued to the TV. The young man glanced at him long enough to roll his eyes, then stare back at the TV. Dunk walked up to Tucker and rubbed his body against his shoes. Not wanting to give the pouting teenager a response, Tucker gently lifted the cat, picked up the jar of milk, and disappeared into his room.

"Hey, Mom," Tucker said into his phone.

"Hi, son," Judith replied.

Tucker could detect from her voice that she was smiling. "How was your day?" he asked.

"The usual. I just stay home all day, babysitting Micah while Jake is off to work and Rebecca insists on going to her store. She has two capable assistants who can more than hold down the fort in her absence, but she still goes." There was a short laugh. "Enough about me. Tell me how your day has gone."

This was one of Tucker's favorite parts of calling Judith. "Well, my day was uneventful. I have two strays now, one cat and a kid. Boy's fourteen. Reminds me of myself at that age."

"Interesting. How did you two meet?"

"I knocked him out."

Judith gasped. "What? Why did you do that?"

Tucker chuckled. "He tried to mug me. That annoyed me, so I disarmed him and knocked him out."

"Clarence!"

"What? I didn't know he was a teenager then, and he had a knife pointed at me."

Judith gasped again.

"Yeah. This all happened yesterday after I left you guys. But I promise, the kid's okay."

"So, you knocked him out and took him home?"

"Yep." Tucker's tone was full of boyishness.

"Chip off the old block."

Tucker laughed. "But Dad didn't knock me out," he said.

"Semantics."

Tucker laughed again. "So, I carried him home. He woke up later and tried to blackmail me."

Judith laughed. "What a boy!"

"Exactly my sentiments. We talked, and I offered to house him. Turned out he didn't have a place to stay. Both parents are dead. His mom from cancer and his dad from a car crash. Doesn't want to go to foster care."

"Poor kid."

"Yeah."

"So how are you guys getting along?"

Tucker laughed before answering. "We are getting along superbly," he said.

"That bad, huh?"

"Not actually. At least not as bad as dad and I were in the first few weeks."

"Alright. What's his name?"

"Dwayne. Dwayne Rodgers."

"Okay. Take good care of him, and Clarence," she said before pausing.

"Yeah, Mom?"

"Be patient with him, alright?"

"Yeah, will do."

"Good."

"Mom, I need a car," Tucker announced.

Judith giggled. "You want me to buy you a car?"

"Nah. More like I need to borrow your car."

"Oh, alright."

"I'm going to see my grandfather tomorrow."

"Oh, that's wonderful." The delight was evident in Judith's voice.

"Yeah. So, I'm going to come steal your car."

"Just be safe."

Tucker laughed.

"What?"

"I've been in wars, escaped bombings, jumped out of airplanes, but you think I won't be safe in a car?"

"It's a mother's job to worry."

"And you do it so well," he said with a smile.

"Whatever. Micah has been asking for you. He was mad when Jake told him you were back."

"Great. Why can't Jake keep his mouth shut?"

"Beats me. So when are you coming over? You'd better have a good explanation for the kid and a minimum of two chocolate bars."

"But Micah doesn't really like chocolate."

"Who said anything about giving them to him?" Judith said.

Tucker laughed.

"Right. Alright Mom, guess I'll be seeing you tomorrow. I love you."

"Goodnight, son. I love you too."

Tucker dropped his cellphone and sprung from the bed, startling Dunk.

"Hey pal, I'm going to Madro tomorrow," Tucker said as he walked to his closet and removed a small bag.

Dunk's eyes followed his every move.

Tucker packed the bag in less than five minutes. After he finished, he had a talk with Dwayne.

"Dwayne!" he hollered, pleased when he heard footsteps a few moments later. "Quit dragging your feet," he said when Dwayne entered the room.

The teenager sat on the bed, still pouting and silent.

"Dwayne, I want you to understand something; it's important you keep away from those 'friends' of yours. I know it isn't easy; I know that from experience. But in the long run, you'll be happy you did it."

"So you want me to betray my friends?"

Betray? What in the world was this kid talking about? Annoyance flared up in Tucker, but Judith's words came to him. Be patient. Breathing in deeply, he continued in a measured voice.

"Dwayne, you have a great sense of loyalty. That's wonderful, and it's a good trait to have. But good things can also be used in bad ways. The loyalty you have for your 'friends', it's misplaced. When you were a mugger and a homeless teen, that feeling of loyalty was natural. But now, you're not that anymore. It's crucial that you understand this, so you don't make mistakes that may be irreversible."

"I'm supposed to just bail on the only people who helped me, because I'm no longer a mugger?"

"Teaching you to steal and threaten people's lives isn't helpful. It might seem like that to you, but I assure you, it isn't." Tucker struggled internally to find calm, but his face showed none. "Look, Dwayne, I lost someone I cared about a lot because of something like this. The same misplaced loyalty you feel is what I felt, and that was what killed him." Tucker closed his eyes. The old familiar pain was rising up.

Dwayne was silent.

"For weeks, he had been telling me to stop my involvement with the gang he rescued me from. But I wouldn't listen, and I still ran odd jobs for them whenever I could. He knew, and he spoke to me about it. I apologized and promised to change, but I didn't." Tucker scoffed. "Apologies don't mean a thing unless you change. I didn't, and on my last job for the gang, I was set up."

Dwayne gaped.

"Surprised? Don't be. Gangs will never leave you alone. Either you are with them, or you're dead. That's the typical M.O. Anyway, I went on that job, and the man who warned me was in the area. He was a cop, so I think he might've been patrolling. He heard the gunshots and charged in without backup."

"That was stupid to do," Dwayne said.

Tucker nodded. "Maybe. But he did it because it was his job. He saw me and I could tell he knew what was going on. He shouted for me to hide, but he got shot trying to cover me and died from his wounds. Wounds he got because of me," Tucker finished.

The room went silent.

"So, you don't want to die protecting me, so I gotta leave my pals?" Dwayne asked.

Tucker narrowed his eyes, but Dwayne spoke before he did. "Kidding," he said with a small grin. "I understand. Thank you for the talk."

Tucker nodded and watched him walk out of the room. "That went pretty well, Dunk."

"Speaking of Dunk, we haven't finished the deal," Dwayne said as he poked his head into the room.

Tucker glanced him over. "A buck an hour," he said.

"Slavery!" Dwayne protested.

Tucker laughed. "Okay, three dollars an hour, no dice."

Dwayne pretended to think about it for a while, then he nodded.

"So, that's seventy-two dollars per day. I'm going to see my grandfather tomorrow, and he isn't a fan of cats. I'll leave Dunk home with you."

"I know. You already told me that."

"By the way, you're paying taxes on your earnings."

Dwayne grumbled his way out of the room.

Tucker smiled as he lay his head on the pillow.

The next morning, he walked into the living area with his bag in hand. He saw Dwayne standing in the kitchen.

"Get Dunk some cat food, and don't forget to buy some milk when you're buying the cat food," he said to the teenager.

"Sure. I won't forget anything."

"You'll get paid when I get back," Tucker said.

"That's not fair at all," Dwayne protested.

"Okay, I'll pay you half now, then half when I'm back."

"Sixty percent now, forty percent when you get back."

"No. I'll pay fifty percent now and fifty when I get back. That's my last offer, or else you'll go back to working for a buck an hour.

Dwayne glared at him. "But you'll be gone the whole weekend. How am I supposed to survive?"

"You will. There's groceries here and some cash left—"

"Yeah, only about ten bucks!" Dwayne interjected.

Tucker placed some cash on the counter. "With the ten bucks and half your pay, you should be able to get whatever you need. Just make sure you get some cat food for Dunk."

Dwayne stalked away. "The cat has more rights than I do," he complained, his arms folded across his chest.

"He came first. Besides, he doesn't wake up late and ask

me questions about what we're eating or not eating. And he doesn't snore."

"Snore?! I don't snore!"

"How would you know?"

"I do not snore," Dwayne insisted.

Tucker shrugged and grinned. The kid was so easy to rile up, it was criminal. "Alright pal, see you," he said before stepping out of the apartment and nearly smacking into Catherine.

"Hi," Catherine's greeting was a nervous one.

"Hey."

They both stared at each other for a moment before Tucker broke the silence.

"So, how have you been?"

"I've been good. Jerry also." She glanced at the bag slung over Tucker's shoulder and it seemed to give her more confidence.

"You running away?" she asked, motioning to his bag.

Tucker chuckled. "No, of course not. I'm going to see my grandfather. He stays in Madro."

"Oh," she said with a smile. "That's nice. Dunk's not going?"

"Nah. Pops hates cats."

"Oh, right." Then she went silent. The previous surge of confidence she had was completely gone.

"I'd better get going. Still gotta get a car before the drive."

"Alright. Take care and be safe."

Tucker nodded and walked down the hallway, aware that she was staring. He wondered if she was staring at his butt and nearly burst into laughter.

He took a cab to the Rowneys' and was there in less than thirty minutes.

He knocked on the old door.

"Coming," came the voice of Judith.

"Hi, handsome," she greeted, while hugging him. She smelled of lavender and powder. She smelled like home.

"Hi Mom." He kissed her cheeks, making her blush with pleasure.

"You are certainly a charmer."

"Learned it from watching Dad charm you," he said as he guided her into the house and shut the door.

She smiled at him.

"Uncle Tucker!" A little boy the size of a baby elephant barreled across the room and launched himself like a torpedo at Tucker. Tucker braced himself for impact.

"Hey little fella, good to see you too," he said, tickling the round little boy.

"Micah, no running, remember?" Rebecca scolded.

"You just get prettier and prettier. Where did you learn it? Do you have sisters?" Tucker joked, making Rebecca blush.

"Oh stop it," she said with a smile and a giggle.

"We have to beg him to come home, and when he finally shows up, he charms my ladies," Jake commented as he walked into the living room.

"That's because you're doing a poor job of it while I'm away," Tucker said.

Rebecca and Judith leaned back, placed their palms over their mouths and made a joint 'ooohhh,' sound.

Jake roared with laughter as he sank into a sofa. "Good one, guys. Tucker, you owe me one."

Tucker glanced around before saying. "Please let that one be a lesson on how to charm ladies. You kinda need it."

Rebecca and Judith repeated their act, making everyone laugh again.

"Excuse us, everyone," Jake said and stood up. "Tucker and I need to have a man-to-man discussion," he finished before pulling a chuckling Tucker along.

They walked to the poolside, and Tucker immediately

knew what Jake intended. He stood closest to the pool, but he didn't let his guard down.

"So, what's up, bro?" Tucker asked, pretending to be serious. He noticed that Jake had shifted most of his weight to his toes and coiled up to spring.

"It's just something I've been trying to figure out!" On the last word, Jake made his move.

Tucker simply moved out of the way and Jake fell headlong into the water. Tucker roared with laughter.

"Hey bro," he started when Jake surfaced. "Never mess with a soldier."

"Oh shut up," Jake said before laughing.

"Give me a hand, would you?" Jake asked, his arm outstretched.

Tucker knew Jake would pull him in and went along with it anyway. When he extended his hand, Jake yanked it. Tucker's feet left the ground, and he smelled a hint of chlorine as he plunged into the cool water.

"Ha! Got you!" Jake shouted when Tucker resurfaced.

Both men had hearty laughs as they climbed out of the pool and walked back into the house.

"I was getting ready to… Oh my goodness, you idiots!" Judith said, bursting into laughter after seeing both of her sons thoroughly soaked.

Micah jumped around and laughed. "I wanna get in water," he said.

"Sure, little man. Next time," Tucker said.

Both men got a change of clothes and dried their wet ones. They walked into Judith's room after freshening up.

"Hey Mom," they both said in tandem.

Judith looked up from an album with tears in her eyes. "I'm a blessed woman," she said, motioning them over.

"Yes, you are a blessed woman, Mom," Jake said.

Tucker nodded and wiped a trail of tears from Judith's cheeks with his thumb.

"You know," Judith began. "When I saw you both enter the house all wet, I was reminded of the times when we all would get into the pool and frolic around without a care in the world. The pool for us was a safe place where nothing else mattered."

"Yes," Jake said, while taking her hand.

Tucker did the same.

"I love you both very much, and I'm glad to be your mother," she said, squeezing each one's palm gently.

"Your relationship reassures me that your father and I did the right things as parents, even though we had no clue what we were doing."

"You guys were the best. Still are," Jake said.

"Yes, absolutely," Tucker agreed.

Judith smiled through her tears and hugged both men.

"Clarence, here's the key you asked for," Judith said a few moments later.

"You're leaving town?" Jake asked.

"Yeah, only for the weekend. I want to see my grandpa."

"And you're taking Mom's car? That old thing?"

Judith smacked him on the head lightly. "You were born in that car."

"Precisely my point. He wouldn't get to Madro till winter," Jake joked.

Tucker laughed.

"That car is faster than you know, Jake," Tucker said with a sly grin.

Jake immediately noticed the grin. "Talk," he commanded.

"Well, Mom had the car's engine changed. The car is now a horse in sheep's clothing."

"Crap."

"Shall we go a quarter-mile?" Tucker proposed with a smile.

"You're on."

"Oh, for goodness' sakes, boys," Judith said, tittering. "No racing till he gets back."

"Mom!" Jake whined like a six-year-old boy.

"Deal," Tucker said.

Judith glanced at Jake.

"Fine, deal," he reluctantly agreed.

The entire family saw Tucker off.

"Drive safe, son. No speeding," Judith warned.

Tucker's response to that was to rev the car's engine. Hard.

"You still feeling lucky, boy?" he asked Jake.

"Talk, talk, talk. We'll settle it when you get back."

After their goodbyes, Tucker drove off.

CHAPTER
EIGHT

The drive to Madro was long, and it afforded Tucker time to think about the past and how things used to be. He remembered growing up in Madro, where he knew everybody. It felt like both a blessing and a curse that he didn't have to live in New York. A blessing because living in a small town meant you knew everyone and every place. A curse because all of your secrets and mistakes were likely known by everyone too.

As the wind whipped his hair in the convertible, Tucker remembered thinking he would never leave the town. But all that changed when his father died. The shame was too much, and not even his grandfather could convince him to stay and ride out the storm. Mr. Rowney always told him that everything in life happened for a reason and had a cause. Tucker wondered what caused him to never know his mother. Or what was the reason for his father marrying an absolute stinker of a woman? As he turned off the freeway, he had the strangest feeling that someone was following him. He pulled over and checked his mirror. There wasn't a single car behind him. He looked around to see if it could be a drone. Nothing. He shrugged and continued onto the road with the feeling of being watched remaining.

When he entered the town, he didn't get a rush of memories like he thought he would. All he got was a feeling of happiness to be back. That was enough, he reasoned. The town hadn't changed one bit. The streets were lined with dried leaves, all the stores still had one name on them, and the pace of the town was slow compared to the not-so-nearby city, New York. He smiled as he made a turn onto Tucker Lane. It felt weird, but reassured him that his grandfather was still the same old Pops, a brash exterior with an inside he once heard his biological father say was softer than a lady's bum. When he got to the gate, he was going to kill the engine and go open it himself, but the gate opened on its own.

That's new, Tucker observed before driving inside. As he stood from the car, Tucker watched the gate close and heard the locks click. He took a moment to survey the expanse of land. He'd always wondered why his grandfather had never sold, despite many buyers and some stupendous offers over the years. *Apart from the stone cottage and the shed next to it, what was there to keep?* he thought. But he reminded himself it was his grandfather's choice. Tucker grabbed his bag and climbed up the stone steps to the tiny cottage that was in the center of a vast expanse of land.

He didn't even bother knocking. He just opened the door and stepped inside. And was met by the barrel of a rifle pointed at his chest.

"State your name and business."

"Pops, it's me," Tucker said.

"Oh, Clarence," his grandfather said as he lowered the rifle.

A moment later, arms like steel beams enveloped Tucker.

"Welcome home, my boy."

"Hi Pops. What's with the rifle?"

"Oh, that. My eyesight is going bad, so I use it to intimidate people."

"What?" Tucker said, chuckling.

"No need to worry, there's no bullets inside. There hasn't been a bullet in it for eleven years now, but no one knows that," the old man said with a wink.

Tucker laugh. *Definitely still the same old Pops.* "Pops, let me see your glasses," he requested before taking them off his grandfather's face.

"Oh, I can see you much better," Pops commented.

Tucker laughed. "Your eyes aren't failing, the glasses are."

"I knew that snarky runt was a quack. I'm going to give him a piece of my mind the next time I see him."

Tucker led his grandfather to a chair.

"Back off, boy. I can pick my own chair," Pops said as he waved him away and sat.

Tucker shook his head and sat beside his grandfather. "So how's it going, Pops?"

"The usual. I wake up by five in the morning—"

Tucker laughed and cut in. "Not that, Pops. I know all about your daily routine. It's been the same for at least twenty-five years."

"Thirty-five," His grandfather corrected and smiled crookedly.

"Right," Tucker said while looking around. "Still the same old cottage, huh? Does Marie still come around?"

"Yes. How else would I keep this cottage spotless?"

Tucker nodded. *It feels good to be here,* he thought. Real good.

"Do you miss the military?" His grandfather said before motioning him to the dining table.

Tucker sighted a cookie jar and picked it up. He grinned at his grandfather as he mimicked the stance of a quarterback.

"Wanna catch, Pops?"

His grandfather chuckled. "You young men think because your flesh is younger, you can do anything. Gimme my cookies."

Tucker opened the cookie jar and offered it to his grandfather.

The old man snatched the entire jar from Tucker, then both men laughed.

"Come on son," his grandfather said while standing to his feet.

Tucker glanced at the ancient wall clock in the cottage. Eight fifteen. Then he remembered.

"Pops, I need to make a call."

"Alright. Meet me outside when you're done."

"Yeah," Tucker said before picking up his bag, removing his phone from it, then dialing.

Moments later, the soft voice of Judith filled his ear.

"Hi Mom."

"Clarence. Finally. I've been worried sick."

"I'm safe, Mom. I got here about ten minutes ago."

"Alright. How is your grandfather?"

"He's fine. Still very strong and healthy, thankfully."

"Okay. Take care, son, alright?"

"Okay, Mom. Good night. Love you."

"Love you too."

The phone clicked off and Tucker ambled outside to join his grandfather at the shed.

"You never answered my question," Pops said.

"Which one?" Tucker asked as he sat.

"Do you miss the military?"

Tucker took a moment to mull it over in his mind. "Yes and no. Yes, because I miss the training, and the thrill of battle, and my brothers in arms and all of it. But then again, I don't miss it because I feel the only reason I went to the military in the first place was to try and repay the debt I owed."

"What debt?"

Tucker held his grandfather's gaze. "The debt I owed to Henry Rowney."

His grandfather nodded sagely. "And now you feel the debt is paid?"

"No. It'll never be. But at least now I know I've gotten that phase out of my system."

His grandfather nodded again. "Alright, good for you, son. So, what next?"

"That's the million-dollar question, Pops. But to be honest, I don't really know. I'm still trying to figure it out."

"Okay. But please don't tell me you're gonna go into private security like most of your military pals are doing."

Tucker laughed. "What's wrong with that, Pops?"

His grandfather merely shrugged and popped a cookie into his mouth. "So, when are you getting a girl?"

"What?"

"You heard me, son."

"A girl? What for?"

Pops chuckled. "Boy, you spent too much time in the military if you're really asking me that."

"Of course I know what a woman is for. But that's not what I need right now, Pops."

"Oh really, what do you need?"

"I need to get my life on track. I need to get a job and figure out what's next."

"And getting yourself a nice, beautiful woman can't be done also?"

"Nah. It'd be a distraction for me."

Tucker's grandfather shook his head. "You young people, you think you have it all figured out. You spend so much time chasing things you think will fulfill you and neglect the one thing no one can really live without in this world."

Tucker was silent for a moment, thinking about what his grandfather said. "Well," he began after a moment. "Maybe I'm chasing after things, but I also know that now is not the time to get hitched. The time for that will come, Pops."

His grandfather studied him for a moment. "You see, Clarence, time is something you can't control."

"Yeah, but—"

"I'm not finished," Pops said sternly. "Don't waste too much time, Clarence."

Tucker suddenly understood. This grandfather still regretted not having enough time with his grandmother.

"Pops." He put his hand on his grandfather's knee and squeezed gently. "I understand what you're saying. I'll get to it soon enough. Just have some things to work through."

His grandfather nodded, his eyes distant and wistful.

"Pops, when was the last time you had bacon?"

"You want Marie to turn me into a turnip?"

Tucker laughed. "She won't know."

His grandfather scoffed. "You really think anything goes on in this town that that woman doesn't know about? Joke's on you."

Tucker felt a challenge coming up. "Pops, you want the bacon or not?"

He observed his grandfather and saw the desire in his eyes. *Bingo*, he thought.

"Don't say I didn't warn you."

Tucker hopped up and dashed to his car, laughing. "You won't be saying that when you have bacon in between your teeth," he hollered back.

A few moments later, he drove from the property, determined to get bacon while eluding the seemingly ubiquitous Marie. He'd missed her also, he thought as he bent into a turn and sped up the road.

She'd always been there, even though his dad seemed to hate her for reasons he didn't know. His dad did a lot of things he didn't understand, he mused as he exited the car. In an attempt to disguise his identity, he wore a cap and dark reflector glasses.

"Evening," he said to the woman at the counter.

"Good evening. What can I get for you?"

"Bacon. Two slabs."

"Coming right up," the woman said, then disappeared. Gregory's was still the same, a small shack-like establishment that had the best service in town with Marie as the manager. Tucker hoped she wouldn't notice him because he had planned to see her the next day.

On Tucker's way back to his grandfather's house, Catherine called him.

"Hi Cathy."

"Hi Tucker. Dwayne said you moved out and he's now the occupant of the apartment."

Tucker laughed. "He just said that so you'd make him dinner. Boy's a natural disaster at cooking."

Catherine laughed. "I'll keep that in mind. So where are you?"

"I'm at my grandfather's. Outside of New York."

"Oh, that's nice. Jerry says hi."

"Tell him I said hi. But let's talk later, alright?"

"Of course. Have a good night."

"You too."

Tucker drove onto his grandfather's property with a triumphant grin.

"Did you get it?" his grandfather asked.

"Did I get it? Of course I did, Pops. And without being seen by Aunt Marie."

"Good. She doesn't need to see you right now. Let's eat. When she comes around to hound me, I'll direct her to you."

"That's not even fair, and you know it," Tucker said, laughing.

"All is fair in food and war. And shut it. I know that's not the correct quote."

Tucker burst into another round of laughter. He'd missed his grandfather. "Let me get the knife," he said before walking into the kitchen. By the time he came back, the first slab of bacon was nearly a quarter gone.

"Pops!" he exclaimed.

"Shut it. I was hungry, and you were taking too long. Now cut up the bacon quickly. Marie could decide to pop up at any minute."

Tucker chuckled at his grandfather's comical make-believe fear of Aunt Marie. She was the sweetest person he knew.

After a hearty dinner, Tucker's grandfather retired to his room and Tucker was left alone with his thoughts. Uncomfortable with the silence in the cottage as his thoughts were too loud, he stepped outside into the night air and went for a walk. The moon bleached surroundings looked ethereal, and as though on autopilot, Tucker walked to the cemetery where his father lay buried.

Arthur C. Tucker
Lived a life.

Tucker sat on a nearby headstone and read the utterly strange pseudo epitaph on his father's grave as questions bounced around in his head like ping-pong balls. *Lived a life? Right. Everyone lives a life.* Suddenly, he got angry. *Why didn't anyone write about the life he lived? Why did he get protection just because he was dead?* Everyone remembered him as a good man who couldn't handle the guilt of killing a man accidentally. But nobody knew that he was drunk when his carelessness killed the sole breadwinner of a family and drove the wife into a depression that led to her death. Nobody knew that he was a father who beat his own son savagely. And after all that, he still got an epitaph that was shrouded in mystery. A mystery that protected him.

Raging, Tucker kicked the gravestone and felt pain strike his foot. He ignored the discomfort and stormed out of the cemetery. When he made it out, he started running. He knew running was the only thing that could keep the voices in his head away, so he ran until he couldn't think anymore. By the time he got back to the cottage, his muscles quivered and perspiration dripped off him like drops of rain.

"I wondered where you ran off to," his grandfather said, seated by the door.

Tucker went to his room without saying a word. He then stripped and had a quick shower before throwing on a change of clothes and walking back to where his grandfather sat.

"It's about him, isn't it?" Pops asked.

"What is?" Tucker asked as he sat.

"The rage I see in your eyes, the emptiness in your soul, the tiredness in your flesh. It's all because of him."

Tucker said nothing.

"Son, no one could tell what kind of man your father was."

Tucker's head went up at that.

"I know you think you know, and that's fine. He, unfortunately, showed you a very terrible part of him, and as his parent, I apologize."

"Grandpa, nothing he did was your fault."

"Boy, everything he did was my fault." The old man paused, swallowed, then continued. "I'm about to tell you some things you never knew about your father. Listen carefully. Growing up, Arthur was a boy who saw me as his role model. A natural tendency, perhaps, but one I was fatally unaware of. He took all I did as the right way to behave, and he never questioned anything I did."

His grandfather paused and glanced down for a moment. When the old man looked back up, his eyes were wet. Tucker winced at the sight and continued listening.

"All that changed the day I sent your grandmother away.

For the first time in his life, he stood up to me and challenged me. What was my response to it? I slapped him," Pops said while holding Tucker's gaze.

"I slapped him that day, and I lost my son forever. I threatened to send him away too, but he did that for me by moving out. At first I thought he was joking, but after a week of not seeing him, I panicked and started searching for him. I found him two weeks later, half-dead in the woods from starvation. I brought him back home and kept him with me." Pops paused again and shut his eyes.

Tucker knew recounting was causing him great pain. "Pops, please stop. I don't need to hear any more."

"No, son, let me finish. I often wondered why I sent Naomi away. I thought it was because of another woman, or because I was having a midlife crisis." Pops chuckled bitterly at that. "I've heard a lot of young men do something unbelievably stupid and then attribute it to having a midlife crisis. It's a load of garbage, and it just tells me that they're irresponsible men, just like I was. The reason I sent Naomi away was because I wanted to break her. You see, my wife was many things, but docile wasn't one of them. She had a mind of her own, and in those days, it was almost criminal for a woman to speak her mind or stand up to her husband. Sure, she taught Arthur to obey me at every turn, but he only did that because she told him to, not because he wanted to. So you see why he flared up when I sent her packing? I thought sending her packing would break her, because I knew just how much she wanted and loved being married. But I was gravely wrong. She left my house with her head held high, and though I didn't realize it at the time, she earned my respect that day." Pops stared at Tucker. "You remind me so much of her. Your defiance, your nobility. You got it from someone, and it sure wasn't from my side of the family," he said with a chuckle.

Tucker forced a smile, digesting everything he was hearing.

"The longer we lived without your grandmother, the more Arthur grew to despise me. I did have another woman, Laura. She was an escort, but that was exactly why I was with her. I flaunted her around town, sure that your grandmother would catch wind of what I was doing. Son, when a woman loves you, never use her love as a weapon. You might just drive her away forever, and let me tell you, war would be a walk in the park compared to what you'll feel. Do you understand?"

Tucker nodded, absorbing every word.

His grandfather cleared his throat and continued. "Naomi heard about everything I was doing, but even that didn't break her. She still came to see Arthur, but she refused to talk to me. Eventually, I understood that she wasn't going to bend for my ego, and when I understood that, I sent Laura away and went on a campaign to get your grandma back. I did win her back, after three grueling years, but by then, your dad was over the legal age and had left. He still saw his mother regularly, but for me, he never spared a minute." Pops took in a labored breath before continuing. "Tucker, your mother is alive."

Tucker's forehead wrinkled. "What?" he said, unsure about what he just heard.

"Yes, son, she's alive. She lives here in Madro, and you already know her."

"Wait. Where? Who is she?" Tucker asked.

"Marie."

"Wait, what? Aunt Marie is my mother?"

"Yes."

Then it all clicked for him. He now understood the reason for the constant gifts, the attention and the love. He remembered asking her why she liked him so much, and he remembered her saying he reminded her of her lost son.

"Is that why she's always been so close to you?" Tucker asked.

His grandfather nodded. "When Arthur told me he'd gotten a girl pregnant, I was mad. When I learned it was Marie, I got even madder. She was the only daughter of her mother, and she was a good girl, according to Naomi. Your grandmother loved her like a daughter, and she always hoped Arthur would eventually see sense and ask to marry her." Pops scoffed. "All Arthur saw was his hatred for me, and as soon as he knew I liked the girl, he hated her. On one of the rare occasions where we spoke more than two words to each other, he informed me he didn't want a goody two shoes like Marie. Rather, he took great pleasure in telling me he was going to marry Lisa, knowing full well that I disapproved of her. I threatened to cut him out of my will, but he just laughed and said he stopped needing anything from me a long time ago."

Tucker's grandfather stood up and headed for the toilet. In his absence, Tucker's mind filled with many thoughts, and he felt he would go mad if he didn't discard them. His grandfather re-entered the room a few minutes later, and the old man's eyes were suspiciously dry.

"After Marie gave birth to you, Arthur took you from her. She begged to see you, but he threatened to kill her if she ever came close. She came to Naomi and me for help, and Naomi told her to stay away till Arthur got his bearings. He never did get them, he only got worse and worse. He raised you alone, refusing help from even Naomi. When you were seven, he married Lisa, and that was the beginning of the end."

Tucker knew very well what his grandfather meant. Life with his father before Lisa was so different than life after her; so much so until he categorized dates in his life to B.L. and A.L., B.L. meaning before Lisa and A.L. meaning after Lisa.

"So you see, son, the kind of man your father was. It was my fault he turned out the way he did, and when he died and you left, I accepted it as my punishment for leading my son wrong." The old man heaved a heavy sigh.

Tucker knew Pops had nothing else to say. He studied his grandfather's wrinkled face intently and spoke after a moment. "Pops, you may be responsible for some of the problems, but you can't blame yourself for all the choices another person makes," he said.

His grandfather smiled broadly, his eyes teary. "That was the exact same thing Naomi said on her deathbed."

"That's because it's true. Whatever you did or didn't do, Dad was a person of his own, and he made his choices," Tucker said.

Aunt Marie, being his mom, changed things. He'd always thought his mother was a callous person to leave him with a monster for a father, but now he knew that she'd never left him at all, not even when her life was threatened.

"Pops, thanks for telling me this," Tucker said as he stood. He helped his grandfather up, and both men retired to their rooms.

The next day, Tucker left the cottage late that morning, and he went into town. Before going to Gregory's, he made a stop at his father's grave, and he stood there, staring.

"Dad, I wish you forgave Grandpa. I wish you accepted Aunt Marie. I wish you didn't do any of the things you did, the alcohol, the abuse, the hatred for Grandpa. I wish you didn't kill that man, and I wish, I wish..." he stuttered, his chest heaving. "Dad, I wish you hadn't killed yourself," he finished before sitting on the stone.

Ten minutes later, he walked out of the cemetery and headed for Gregory's. When he got to the restaurant, he took a seat at the back and watched for Aunt Marie. After watching for about ten minutes, he saw her. She was carrying a large tray and laughing in mid-stride. She looked very serene.

Tucker smiled. He'd thought he didn't have a mother, but he was wrong. He just hadn't known. Now he had two mothers, and he suddenly couldn't wait for them to meet. He smiled when she sighted him and came running.

"Clarence," she said. Her brown eyes were doe soft with maternal love.

"Hi Mom," he said, watching her face as it went from smiling to puzzled to comprehension and then to shock.

"You... you... know?" The question was a breathless whisper.

"Yes. Grandpa told me yesterday. He told me everything."

She smiled and sat with him, staring hard at his face.

"You've been there my whole life, and I thought I'd never know my biological mother."

Marie smiled and wiped away her tears.

"Mom, I'm sorry for all that happened."

"You've got nothing to be sorry for, Clarence. Nothing. You've always been the one person I could afford to love without the fear of that love never returning."

"I love you, Mom. I know we've lost so much time, but we still have a lot of time, alright?"

Marie nodded hopefully.

"I love you too, Clarence. I've waited for this day for years and had lost all hope that it'd ever come. I'm so happy," she said, smiling.

"Me too. I have so much to tell you, but it seems the restaurant is filling up fast and they might need you," Tucker said, glancing around the dining room as a mob of customers entered. "What time does your shift end?"

Marie laughed. "I don't have a shift, sweetie. I'm the owner."

"I know. But today, you do have a shift. I want to spend

time with my mom, and nothing is stopping me," Tucker said.

Marie laughed again. "Alright. I'll be out by six."

"Sweet. Will you come over to the cottage?"

Marie's face suddenly became serious. "Oh, you best believe I will. I have to warn Mark against eating bacon. A reliable source informed me that a young man came here yesterday to get two slabs of bacon and ferried it to the Tucker cottage in his snarky convertible."

Tucker laughed. "Snarky convertible?"

"Not my words."

"Right. Okay, I'll let you get back to work. I love you, Mom."

Marie smiled. "I love you too, son."

Tucker stood and embraced her. "And Mom," he said after releasing her from the hug, "I have two moms now."

"How did that happen?" Marie said, giggling.

"You'll find out after your shift," Tucker said.

CHAPTER
NINE

"And that's how he became one of my best friends," Tucker finished.

Marie clapped excitedly while his grandfather chuckled.

"So, son, this Pozo, where is he now?" she asked.

"He stays in his grandma's basement back in New York. He says he has a decade of gaming to catch up with," Tucker replied as he shook his head and smiled.

Marie smiled. "I'd say he's right."

After Tucker's grandfather had retired to his room, Tucker and Marie went outside to sit in the shed.

"You know, I used to dream I'd get to tell you stories here," Marie said.

"You can tell me all the stories you want now, Mom."

She laughed shortly. "I'm afraid you've outgrown a lot of the stories I had in mind. But if you want, I have hundreds of recipes in my head I can share. I really should write them all down one of these days."

Tucker was quiet and pensive.

"What's wrong, Clarence?"

He glanced at her. "I'm trying to figure out what to do

next. A lot of my pals are going into private security and all that, but it's really not my thing."

Marie tilted her head slightly to the left, studied Tucker's face and squinted. "Do you still enjoy cooking?"

Tucker was a bit baffled. "Yeah. What does that got to do with this?"

"Patience. You still enjoy cooking, and according to your stories, you're very good at it. A good number of the recipes I use now were made by you unintentionally when you worked with me during your summer vacations. So I say why not look into it now? It seemed to be your passion then, and I think it still is."

"Funny, I've never thought of that. Thanks, Mom."

Marie nodded and smiled. "So, next topic—let me see," she said as she rolled her eyes slowly. "Yep. Is there a girl?"

"What? Mom!"

"What?" she asked, smiling sweetly. "You're a good-looking young man who needs a wife."

"What? You're unbelievable," he said with a chuckle.

"No, she isn't. She's right, or do you want to wait till I'm in my grave before bringing me a kid to bounce on my knees?" Pops said from behind him and winked at Marie, who laughed.

"Pops!" Tucker exclaimed.

His grandfather laughed. "You young people think you're the only ones who can sneak around," the old man said as he sat.

"Alright, I see what this is. You guys are trying to corner me," Tucker said.

"So? It's about time, don't you think?" Marie pressed.

Tucker narrowed his eyes, and Marie laughed.

"That's not going to work now. I've been immune to that since you were ten," she said.

Tucker laughed. "Alright, alright. No, there's no girl, and yes, I'll let you know if there is."

"If?" his grandfather complained.

"Yeah, if. That's what you get for trying to corner me," Tucker said, enjoying himself.

"Don't mind him, Pops. He's just messing with you. There's a girl, he just don't want to bring her home yet," Marie said, and giggled when Tucker frowned at her. "C'mon Clarence, admit it."

"There's nothing to admit. Case closed," Tucker said. "Let's talk about something else."

"Okay. What about becoming a chef? You would be absolutely excellent at it," Marie suggested again.

"I think that might work," Tucker agreed.

"Then, in that case, how much do you need to start your restaurant?" Pops asked.

Marie gasped.

"Pops, we talked about this. Let me figure it out myself. Let me carve my own path," Tucker said, a hint of frustration in his voice.

"Alright, alright," his grandfather agreed reluctantly.

An idea sprang up in Tucker's mind. "Pops, could you do something for me?"

"Go," his grandfather said.

"Could you loan Mom some money so she could expand Gregory's?"

"Clarence!" his mother raised her tone, clearly shocked.

"Done," Pops said. "But on one condition."

Tucker eyed his grandfather, on guard for what was about to come. "Which is?"

"Please, son, let me make some calls. As a Tucker, you shouldn't work in just any restaurant. I won't tell them to give you a job, just to put in a good word for you," Pops pleaded while looking at his grandson with a glimmer of hope in his eyes.

Tucker looked at his mother and she nodded softly, smiling. He heaved a sigh.

"Alright Pops. Make your calls. But don't tell them to give me a job just because I'm your grandson. I want to make my own way."

"Alright son," Pops said and removed his cell from his pajamas pocket as he stood up. He returned to the shed a moment later, smiling crookedly. "You'll get an email soon about an interview. Do whatever it says," he said before kissing Marie's cheek, hugging Tucker, and going back into the cottage.

"He looked so peaceful. Thank you, Clarence," Marie said.

Tucker nodded and hugged his mother, breathing in her honeysuckle fragrance.

"I wish we had more time," she said.

"We do. I'm goin' back to New York, but I'll be back here next week, alright?" he said as he held her at arm's length.

She nodded and pulled his cheeks playfully. "Drive safe when you leave."

Tucker rolled his eyes and smiled. "Same thing Mrs. Rowney said."

"See? We haven't even met, yet, but both your moms worry about you."

"And y'all do it so well."

As Tucker dressed up for the interview on Thursday morning, he thought about the box his adopted mother, Judith, had given him. He held it in his hands and was about to open it, but a feeling that he shouldn't overwhelmed him, so he didn't. Maybe it contained a secret, maybe a riddle, or a case to crack. Or it could just be a love letter, Tucker thought. Admitting that he couldn't predict what was inside, he tightened his belt and looked at himself one final time in the mirror.

"Dunk," he called and listened for the cat to respond.

When he didn't, Tucker went to the living room and saw Dunk eating the last of his food.

"I knew you had to be eating," he snarled. "That's all you do. Oh yeah, apart from sleeping."

The cat meowed and raised its head. As if inspecting Tucker, he ran his colored eyes the length of the tall man and meowed his compliment.

"You didn't have to tell me. I know I look good," Tucker said before picking up the keys to Judith's car and heading for the door. "Don't do anything I wouldn't do, Dunk. Remember, Mrs. Mary's army is still looking for cats," he said before closing the door.

Thoughts of Dwayne crossed his mind as he left his apartment. Dwayne will be fine, he reassured himself. It was only a matter of time before the boy would cut off his old ways of living. *I hope it's not too late by then*, Tucker retorted at his own thoughts as he walked to the car. Well, Dwayne has to decide what is right for himself. Tucker kept reminding himself of that and hoped the young man would change soon.

Tucker raised the volume of the car's stereo and started on his trip to Lola's Farm to Table. He loved listening to old school R&B. It kept him calm and helped him to think. He figured he would arrive at the interview about fifteen minutes early, which was the perfect time to get there.

The bright smile he got from the female at the door startled him for a second, but then he figured she thought he was a customer and was just giving him a warm welcome. Her smile was in direct contrast with the thick frown on the manager's face when he walked in. The man was scolding a cook.

"Do come in, Mr. Tucker, and have a seat," the manager said.

Tucker nodded and sat in one of the office's chairs. From the look of the expensive mahogany and wall paintings, Tucker concluded the restaurant had to be doing well, which was a good thing. Another woman came to the manager's office just when his interview was about to begin. The manager introduced her as the CEO. Tucker got up and shook her soft, wrinkled hand before sitting back down.

"How's Grandpa Tucker these days?" the woman asked. She had silver hair and Tucker figured she had to be close to seventy.

"The old man is doing great, and thanks for asking, ma'am," he said.

With much detail, Tucker explained his love for food and cooking and how he had volunteered at a local kitchen while in the military. Ms. Faye, the CEO, explained they needed someone to make new and exciting dishes their customers would enjoy.

"We want to do better by our customers in the coming year, and we need a talented chef."

"You won't regret taking me on, ma'am," Tucker said.

The interview went on for about an hour before they finally agreed on work hours and pay. Tucker thanked Ms. Faye and the manager. He'd have to call his grandfather and tell him about it.

Tucker entered the car and fired up the engine. "Phew!" he sighed as he turned the music back on and hit the gas.

"Shut up, Dunk," Tucker said as he stepped into the room. The feline was in a playful mood, prancing about, stretching intermittently and staring at any and every object in Tucker's room.

"Are you going bonkers on me again? Because if you are, I'll donate you to Mrs. Mary and her army of cats. Let's see how you'll like cat military," Tucker threatened.

The cat merely stared at him for a moment before hopping

on the bed, circling his shirt and lying down on it, tail twitching gently.

"Get off my shirt you..." Tucker started before hearing a sharp noise from outside his apartment.

He threw a pair of shorts on, draped his towel around his neck, and hurried to his door. As he opened the door and stepped out, a dark-skinned, bald, stocky man with flared nostrils and gritted teeth brushed by him. The man muttered under his breath as he stalked down the hall with a stack of papers in hand.

Tucker glanced at Catherine's door and heard whimpering. A bit concerned, he entered the apartment and his mouth fell open at what he saw. Inside, chairs lay flipped over, dishes and containers littered the kitchen countertops, and Catherine sat on the floor, crying. Jerry stared, his face a mask of nothingness. Rage rose in Tucker's gut as he comprehended what had happened. He considered going after the man, but one look at Jerry's face and he stayed instead.

Tucker crouched beside Catherine. "Catherine, what happened? Did he hit you? Are you okay?"

Catherine simply nodded and continued weeping softly. He'd fought countless insurgents, killed a couple of them, assisted hundreds of locals in getting to safety, and buried a few, but none of that prepared him for how undone he felt as Catherine wept. He glanced at Jerry, who was curled up in a corner, silent and staring into space.

Tucker bit down on the wave of fury and took in a deep breath. "Catherine," he said in a soft tone.

Catherine looked up at him, her eyes misty and red.

"I'm sorry for this. Can I get you anything?"

Catherine shook her head and continued crying.

"What did you do?" came a voice from the door.

Tucker turned and saw Dwayne staring at him with squinted eyes.

"Come inside and help her," Tucker said.

Dwayne's voice became harder. "What did you do to her?"

"I didn't do anything. Just come in and help," Tucker instructed, a bit irritated.

"He didn't do anything wrong," Catherine said softly.

Dwayne nodded and scampered towards her. "Who did this?" he demanded.

"That's not any of your business. What is your business now is to help me rearrange her apartment," Tucker said.

"You don't tell me what to do. You're not my da—" Dwayne started.

"Look," Tucker interrupted him. "I don't have the time or patience for this teenage tantrum. Either you make yourself useful or you get lost."

Dwayne's face was still flinty, but his lips quirked a bit. "What do I need to do?"

"Turn those chairs right side up," Tucker said, pointing to three chairs. "Then straighten up the kitchen, but watch for glass as you're cleaning up. Try and gather the shards of glass together and dispose of them. You'll know your next assignment when you're done," Tucker finished before helping Catherine up.

Dwayne immediately got to work while Tucker led Catherine out of her apartment and into his. "Sit here. We'll work on straightening your apartment, alright."

Catherine nodded gently. "Jerry?"

"Yes. I'll go get him now," Tucker said before leaving his apartment and entering hers.

"Hey kiddo," Tucker said as he crouched in front of Jerry.

The boy had his elbows tucked in and his eyes were wide. "Hey," he mumbled with his arms folded and shaking.

Tucker gritted his teeth. *What kind of man would do this to a kid,* he wondered. "Mommy wants to see you. Wanna go?"

Jerry looked up and into Tucker's eyes. "Will the bad man come again?"

"No, the bad man won't come again, alright?"

The boy nodded.

"Now, let's go meet Mommy."

Tucker stretched out a palm and the boy took it. His small hand disappeared inside of Tucker's larger one. Gently, Tucker walked the boy out of the apartment and into his own. As the mother and son hugged, Tucker smiled.

Almost an hour later, Tucker felt Catherine's apartment was once again safe to occupy.

"If that man comes again, I will…" Dwayne asserted.

"You'll do what exactly?" Tucker said, the control over his fury slipping a bit.

Dwayne seemed to recognize it and wisely kept his mouth shut.

"If he comes around again, stay low, call the cops," Tucker said.

Dwayne scoffed. "The cops? They never do anything right, man."

"Well, call them. Don't try to take him on yourself. You saw what he did to the house."

"I'm tougher than the house," Dwayne boasted.

Tucker delivered a quick jab to his stomach and dropped the boy. "Tougher? Nah," Tucker said.

Dwayne writhed on the floor and refused Tucker's hand to help him up.

"Thank you. I don't know what I'd have done without you both today," Catherine said back at Tucker's apartment.

Tucker nodded and smiled.

Dwayne's eyebrows raised. "I'm hungry," he mentioned casually.

Tucker squinted at the young man.

Catherine hesitated a bit and looked at Tucker. Unable to read his expression, she turned to Dwayne. "What would you like for dinner?"

"Fish casserole."

Catherine smiled and nodded, then picked up Jerry and walked out of the apartment.

Tucker waited until Dwayne closed the door before speaking.

"What's your problem, runt?"

Dwayne narrowed his eyes. "Quit calling me that."

Tucker came closer and stared him down. "Runt, I just asked you, what is your problem?"

Dwayne's expression became hard. "Stop calling me that."

"I'll stop when you mature," Tucker said before turning away. "What does he think he's doing, asking the neighbor for food?" Tucker asked Dunk.

The cat twitched its tail in agreement.

"Exactly my point. He could've just asked me, rather he chose to play smart and ask the neighbor. A woman who has had a rough day," he said, and the cat meowed in support.

"Catherine is here," Dwayne said, his head poking into Tucker's room.

Tucker barely looked up from his book.

Dwayne sighed and stepped into the room. "Look, man, I'm sorry about asking her for food. I just wanted the casserole again."

Tucker studied the boy for a moment. "Alright, it's fine. Just don't let it happen again."

"Yep," Dwayne said before leaving the room.

Tucker left Dunk to sleep and walked into the living room.

"Hey Catherine."

"Cathy. Isn't Catherine too long to call every time?" she asked with a small smile.

"Cathy then," Tucker said.

"As a way of thanking you guys for your help earlier today, I wanted to invite you over for dinner. It's nothing special, just fish casserole," Catherine said before smiling at Dwayne.

"Cathy, you don't have to go through the trouble," Tucker said.

"It's no trouble at all. Please, let me thank you."

Not wanting to disappoint her, Tucker nodded while Dwayne tried not to look too pleased. A few minutes later, all four of them sat around Catherine's table and Jerry said grace.

"Alright everyone, time to dig in," Catherine said.

Dwayne finished his meal and asked for more. Catherine obliged happily, grabbing his plate and piling more casserole on top of it. Tucker focused on his food and refused to let Dwayne's lack of manner affect him. He knew the boy was trying to lock his gaze, but he avoided him and told Catherine that her food tasted excellent instead.

Tucker turned his attention to Jerry. "Hey kiddo," he called in a playful voice.

Catherine smiled.

"Do you like your food?" Tucker continued.

Jerry nodded.

Catherine patted her son's head, but he wasn't budging.

Tucker watched the little boy. "How about you play with Dunk?" he said. "Would you like to give him some fish? Cats like fish."

Jerry nodded, and his face lit up.

Tucker stood and moved Jerry's chair backwards, giving the boy room to step down from his seat. He then winked at Catherine before taking Jerry to his apartment.

"Hey, Dunk," Tucker called. "Someone's here to see you."

Dunk came out from behind the sofa and meowed. He circled the little boy and meowed.

Tucker smiled. "He remembers you," he told Jerry.

Jerry bent and opened his palm, where he held a small squashed piece of fish.

Dunk smelled it and looked at Tucker, then back at Jerry. He did a final quality assurance check before eating the fish out of the little boy's hand. He licked his palm to say thank you and wriggled his tail. Jerry smiled and let Dunk climb on his shoulder. Soon, he mimicked Dunk every time he meowed, until it seemed they were taking turns at it.

Tucker watched them play hide and seek and decided to let the boy play until he was tired.

Moments later, the door squeaked open and Dwayne came in with Catherine.

"Ooooh," Catherine giggled at the hopping and bubbling Jerry. "Playing with Dunk now, are we?"

"He's a great cat, Mom," Jerry panted.

"Of course, I mean he stays with Tucker," Dwayne remarked and finally got Tucker's attention. It was not more than a moment's stare and Tucker lost interest again. He was trying to be patient with the teenager, but there was only so much a man could take.

"Would you like some coffee?" Tucker asked Catherine.

She shook her head. "No thanks. I've already taken a good part of your time today and I think you need to rest. Thank you for everything."

Tucker merely nodded and looked around for Jerry. He caught him from behind and lifted him into the air.

Jerry cackled in excitement and yelled, "Uncle Tuck, higher!"

Catherine collected him and thanked Tucker again. She kissed Dwayne's forehead and left.

Dwayne bolted the door and waited for Tucker to speak. "Why are you ignoring me?" he finally asked Tucker.

Tucker looked straight at him. "Because I'm done with your stubbornness."

Dwayne frowned. "I'll go if you want me to."

"I'm not begging you to stay!" Tucker said. "If you think you're doing me a favor by staying, you need to think again." Tucker ignored Judith's voice screaming in his head. *Be patient with him.*

"What did I do?" Dwayne asked.

Tucker shook his head. "You don't guilt trip me, runt. You know exactly what you did. And until you start acting like a mature person, I won't treat you like one."

Tucker left Dwayne in the living room. He snatched a shaving stick from the pack in the bathroom and scolded himself for losing his patience.

"I can't be exactly like you, Dad. I'm not as patient as you were," he mumbled, thinking of his father, Mr. Rowney.

"Give him time, son," he heard Judith say.

How much more time? Dwayne was staying loyal to his 'friends', who only wanted to take all they could from him.

"It's the only family he's ever known," Judith's voice replied.

And a terrible first family too! Tucker groaned. He brushed his teeth and took a shower. By the time he came back out, Dwayne was gone.

The next couple of days passed without incident for Tucker. He got a response from the interview and they wanted him to start the following week. Catherine and Jerry said hello to him in the evenings, and Tucker avoided bringing up the topic about the other day to Catherine. The man was obviously her husband, who she didn't want anymore, but he decided he'd keep his nose out of it.

Tucker called his grandfather to thank him for the referral, then ordered a cookbook he always planned to buy from

Amazon. He added a bag of cat food to the order and informed Dunk he was serious about reducing his milk.

"I'll only give milk to someone who can cook, clean, and talk to me," Tucker said.

Dunk had no problems with it. He meowed his agreement and rubbed himself against Tucker's feet.

Tucker felt no nervousness as he dressed for work the following Monday. He realized again that the challenges he had taken on in the military had made him immune to being afraid of pretty much anything.

As he drove from downtown, he thought about Dwayne. He felt he told the teenager everything he was supposed to and wouldn't stand for the boy bouncing between his house and the streets. The time had finally come for Dwayne to choose one and stick with it. Tucker was happy they finally had that talk. Now he was sure of one thing, either Dwayne returns to stay for good, or he leaves and doesn't come back. Tucker prepared himself for either of the two. Dwayne could no longer come and go as he pleased. No, if he's going to stay, there are rules. Rules that the young man would have to obey. Just like Dunk.

Tucker spent the first day of work getting to know the organization and how things were done. He was glad to find that the manager liked his food and approved him to cook for the customers on the following day. His shift ended at 9 pm, and he drove home with a light heart. He realized some merits of working as a chef—he'd eat out less because the restaurant provided a free meal to staff members every day. As he killed the car's engine, he noticed his apartment's lights were on. Dwayne, he thought. This better be good. Tucker carried the bag of food he brought with him from the restaurant and opened the door to find Dwayne,

Catherine, and Jerry inside. Dwayne had a bloodied eye. Catherine held the young man's chin while inspecting the injury.

"What's going on here?" Tucker asked, assuming Dwayne had gotten into a street fight.

"I'm sorry, Tucker, this is all my fault," Catherine sobbed.

"What happened?" Tucker asked again while placing the bag on the table.

"The bad man came back," Jerry said.

Tucker couldn't believe his ears. "What! Dwayne, what happened?"

Dwayne sat up. "I came home to see you and met him harassing Catherine."

"You took him on, didn't you?" Tucker asked Dwayne.

"He was going to beat—"

"I told you not to take him on!" Tucker hit the table. "You should've called me."

"Tucker, please, it was all my fault," Catherine cried again.

Tucker breathed gently to calm himself. "Okay," he said. "Okay." He looked around. "Where's Dunk?"

"In his box," Jerry said.

Tucker nodded and moved closer to examine Dwayne. "It's alright, Catherine, I'll take care of it."

Catherine shook her head. "Please let me clean him up."

"No," Tucker said firmly. "I'll do it. And I want to know what that guy wants with you."

Catherine nodded.

"I mean it."

"Okay," she said, her voice cracking.

Tucker stared at her for a moment, then sighed. "But for now, you should go to your apartment and clean yourself up," he told her.

"Can I stay here?" Jerry asked no one in particular.

Tucker looked at Catherine and signaled for her to make the call.

"It's alright, pumpkin. I'll bring you a milkshake, okay?" she answered.

Jerry nodded and sat with Dwayne and Tucker.

"It's alright," Tucker said calmly, noticing that Dwayne was afraid he'd scold him again. "I don't blame you, Dwayne. I just want you to be safe. If anything ever happened to you because you met me, I'll never forgive myself."

Dwayne shook his head and tried to open his bloodied eye. "It's because of you, Tucker, that nothing bad is gonna happen to me."

Tucker was unprepared for the hug that enveloped him, nearly making him cringe at the tightness. It felt like Officer Rowney hugging him when he was younger.

"Are we good?" Tucker asked when Dwayne released him.

"Yes."

Catherine entered the apartment holding two bottles. "Here, have a milkshake, Dwayne," she said while extending a bottle toward him.

Dwayne shook his head. "No thanks."

Tucker winced, then shook his head. In all the time he had known Dwayne, he never saw the young man refuse free food.

"What's wrong?" Tucker asked.

"I'm somewhat lactose intolerant," Dwayne explained. "I mean, it's not real bad, but having a direct shot of milk like that would mess up my stomach."

"Right," Tucker said with a nod. "Sorry about that, pal."

Catherine smiled and passed Jerry his milkshake.

Tucker got a bowl of warm water and a towel and cleaned up Dwayne's face. He applied some antiseptic to the wounds and told him to use some pain relievers. "I brought some food from the restaurant. You can have it," Tucker told him.

"How was your first day?" Dwayne asked, washing his hands in the bowl Tucker brought.

Tucker smiled. "I'm enjoying it so far. So I'm optimistic."

Dwayne smiled back.

Catherine had gone out again, this time with Jerry. He wanted to use the bathroom. Tucker and Dwayne were alone.

"I'll cook, I'll clean, I'll do anything, Tucker. Please let me stay with you," Dwayne continued, looking straight at Tucker.

Tucker realized again why he liked Dwayne. Take away the teenage tantrums and naivety, and Dwayne was a fearless kid.

"And feed the cat," Tucker added, trying to sound mean.

Dwayne nodded. "And feed the cat."

Tucker smiled. "I'll get your food ready. But listen," he said as he stood up. "All I need is for you to be responsible. That's all I ask. You do your part, I'll do mine."

"I promise," Dwayne said.

Tucker, not fully convinced, asked, "Are you still going to bail on me and go see your friends?"

Dwayne shook his head. "They're not my friends."

"How do you know that?"

"They tried to talk me out of coming to stay with you. They said having a home didn't mean having a good future."

Tucker nodded.

"So," Dwayne continued. "I figured anyone who really loved me wouldn't want me to miss a chance to stay with an amazing war hero."

Tucker twitched. "Did you tell them I'm ex-military?"

"No, Tucker. I promised you I wouldn't. But I told them how smart you are."

Tucker smiled. He put some food on Dwayne's plate and told him to come eat.

Dunk came out of his hiding place at the smell of food and growled at Dwayne.

"He's always hungry. I don't know how," Tucker said.

Dwayne laughed. "Sounds like me."

Tucker looked around. "Did you come with anything?" he asked Dwayne.

"I have some clothes in that bag," Dwayne pointed to a small, shabby backpack. "There's a diary there too. That's all I have."

Tucker raised an eyebrow. "You keep a diary?"

"Yeah, I know how to write," Dwayne replied.

Tucker swooped at the boy's head.

Dwayne laughed and leaned away.

"We're going shopping tomorrow," Tucker told him. "And I'll tell Catherine to find a school for you."

Dwayne nodded. "Thank you. I don't deserve this."

"I just need you to take care of yourself, Dwayne."

"I will," Dwayne assured.

When they turned in that night, Tucker collected his thoughts and opened the box from Rowney for the first time. A smile arched on his face and took away the sting from the headache he had.

"The old fox," Tucker muttered, genuinely amused.

Violence is not always the answer. Try caring. Yeah, right, Tucker muttered as a quote he had read from a note in the box came to mind when he woke up the next day. He definitely needed it, he told himself. He needed it to stop from finding and beating the low-life Catherine married. Tucker knew it wouldn't end well for the guy if he ever saw him again. Especially since the man had now put his hands on Dwayne too, but Rowney's written words held Tucker. It was six in the morning. He threw on a pair of shorts and walked to the bathroom to brush his teeth. The apartment was quiet and he could hear Dwayne snoring. Having gone to sleep late the previous night, he told himself to go back to bed, but he knew that wasn't happening. The thorough training from the military and all the danger they had to evade turned him into an entirely different person. He wondered if he would still be the same if he had a woman in his life.

Catherine flashed to his mind. He scoffed as he began scrubbing his teeth with the hard bristles before calming down. He decided not to go after the buffoon yet, but he ached with a burning desire to confront the man.

"No, I just want to talk to him," Tucker said to his reflec-

tion in the mirror. "Just to talk. Maybe he'd have an explanation for what's wrong with him and why he had to hit my
friend and my—" He stopped. Yeah, Dwayne. What's the boy
to him now?

Tucker laughed at himself. "No, he's not my son yet," he
told his accusing image. "More like my friend. Rowney never
called me his father. I chose him. I'd have to let Dwayne do
the same." His image pouted at him and he shrugged. "It's a
no-brainer, actually."

"Who are you talking to?" Dwayne asked while yawning.

Tucker jumped at the question.

Dwayne laughed. "I didn't know ex-military soldiers get
startled so easily," he said, still laughing.

"Watch your mouth," Tucker aimed the toothbrush at him.

"Ooops," Dwayne dodged. "Looks like someone woke up
grumpy."

"Why are you up, anyway? You should still be in bed. I
added a sleeping pill to your medicine last night to keep you
silent for a little longer today."

Dwayne laughed. "You wouldn't dare."

Tucker cleaned his face with a towel and looked at
Dwayne sternly. "Yeah, I didn't do it last night, but don't
tempt me. I might do it today."

He brushed against Dwayne as he left the bathroom.
Dwayne sniggered as he left, but Tucker ignored him. Tucker
went to the living room and Dwayne returned from the bathroom with speed.

"What's your morning routine here?" he asked Tucker.

Tucker shrugged. "Eat and go out, I guess. Take it as it
comes."

Dwayne nodded. "Could you buy a vacuum cleaner?"

"Sure, why not? All you have to do is give me the cash,"
Tucker teased.

Dwayne laughed again.

Tucker knew the young man was enjoying himself. "Let's

go shopping this morning. My shift starts at two and I have some things to do before then."

"Okay," Dwayne said as he picked up the trash to take it outside.

When Tucker and Dwayne came back from shopping, Catherine made them lunch. Tucker expressed to her how much he enjoyed it before leading her to his apartment while Dwayne stayed in her unit with Jerry.

"Can you find a school for Dwayne, Catherine?" Tucker said when the two were sitting alone on his sofa.

Catherine frowned and nodded.

"What?" Tucker asked.

"It's a really noble thing you've done for Dwayne."

"Yeah? But I couldn't have done anything different. The kid is trying to be somebody." Tucker replied, a knot growing in his chest as he remembered his younger self.

"You are such a kind man, Tucker. Thank you for everything."

Tucker looked straight at Catherine for a long moment and noticed for the first time that she had green eyes.

"You have beautiful eyes," he said softly and unsure if it came out as he intended.

"It's very lovely to hear you say that to me," she said, returning the stare.

"Let me know when you find a school for my boy. Thanks for lunch," Tucker said as he quickly stood.

Catherine took the cue and wished him a good day at work.

Tucker was beside himself with worry and fear as he dressed for work. He was noticing Catherine. He had to admit that she was beautiful. Her oval face and high cheekbones had him stunned for the third time in twenty-four hours. He didn't realize what her wet face the previous night did to him until the next morning when he woke up with rage in his heart and ached to twist her husband's neck. Ex-husband. Whatever.

Mom, I think I'm falling for her. He sent the quick text to Judith and turned off his phone. He needed time to think and clear his head before he did anything stupid. Tucker gave Dwayne instructions to call him if anything came up, especially if Catherine's husband showed up, then gave the young man some cash before leaving for work.

His mind, for the rest of the day, was filled with thoughts of Catherine. *No, man. This is happening all too fast*. He cautioned himself. He had been in town for only a few weeks and couldn't be with a woman. Too soon to fall for her. He had no time for the distractions, uncertainty, or challenges that came with loving someone. *Not Clair, not Rosie, not Miriam, and now not Catherine? Who's it ever gonna be?* He shook his head to dismiss his thoughts. That's right, there was Clair. That was a very long time ago. She was like Catherine, but she didn't have a child, and definitely not an abusive husband. How did Catherine wind up with that man? He had asked himself the question over and over. Even Catherine didn't know how she ended up with such a crazy man, he was thinking. What's to say she wasn't still in love with him?

His father was in a relationship with a terrible woman and he still loved her. That's why the man came up with the terrible saying: *Love a woman, give her your all and watch her throw it all back in your face*. Those were his father's exact words every day when Lisa left him for another loser. His father never left her because he said he loved her too much, something Tucker didn't understand even as a boy. After his father found her cheating on him three different times and survived one of her attempts to poison him, Tucker knew it was wise to stay away from her, away from them. Because his old man had literally become a slave to the woman. For love. How do you love someone who doesn't even love you? Tucker cringed as he thought about everything. He wasn't willing to give his heart to someone who would take it and make a mess of it. Not Catherine. Not Catherine? How would he even know that? There's no formula to these things. But Catherine is not Lisa. Pffft. How would he know?

Judith's call came in on his way back from work that evening.

"Hello, beautiful," Tucker answered the phone.

"Hey, handsome, how was your day?" Judith replied in a delightful tone.

"Wonderful. You got my text, uh?"

"Yeah, I did."

Tucker put her on hold and pulled over to continue the call. "I'm loving your car, yeah, but I'll return it soon."

"Stop it," Judith said. "Take all the time you need, sweetheart. I insist."

"Well, how can I refuse a beautiful woman's request?" Tucker said, knowing he had set himself up.

"And speaking of beautiful women," Judith began.

Tucker smiled. She fell for the trap.

"What's your fear about her?" Judith continued.

Tucker resisted the urge to laugh and just smiled instead.

"First, I never said she was beautiful. Second, I didn't say I had any fear."

"Both your rebuttals are very untrue, and you know me too well, so talk to me, Clarence."

"Okay. I just think I may have a repeat of my father's life, you know, my biological father. He loved a monster."

"That fear will do you no good, son. You're not your father, and Catherine is not the *monster* your father loved. You have to understand that. Don't let fear of the unknown keep you from moving forward, my dear."

Tucker nodded. If only it was that simple. "Yes, Mom," he said.

"I know you're on your way home now. We'll talk about this when you're well rested."

"That's perfect. How's Becca?"

"Oh, she's great. You should call her."

"I'll do that, beautiful."

"Talk to you soon. Love you."

"Love you right back."

A minute after Tucker hung up, the phone rang, but this time it was an unknown number. He ignored the call, figuring it was a telemarketer or someone wanting to sell him something. Moments later, the phone beeped. When he looked at the screen, he saw a text message, *We'll speak soon.*

Tucker shook his head and deleted the text message. "Not if I can help it," he muttered before yawning and focusing on the road.

The next couple of days rolled by really fast. Dwayne was settling into his new school, and Tucker had considered moving both of them into a new apartment. The trio of him, Dunk, and Dwayne, was becoming too much for one little apartment. He held the thought in his heart and decided to wait and see how things would go. Dwayne found a job as a waiter after school. And although he worked four-hour shifts, his performance in school didn't suffer at all. One day after he came home from work, the young man wanted to discuss helping Tucker with the bills.

"No, absolutely not," Tucker disagreed.

"What happened to me being responsible?"

"Nothing. It just doesn't mean you get to pay rent or split the utilities. You are still in high school. Save a lot, but spend too and enjoy yourself. You won't be in high school forever."

There was absolutely no way he'd let the boy touch any of the bills. He was the grownup and would take care of both Dwayne and Dunk.

Tucker found himself avoiding Catherine. He attributed it all to wanting to get his head straight. The young, beautiful woman was not clingy and Tucker appreciated that, but she still brought him food, which he mostly passed on to Dwayne and Dunk. He knew she wanted something more, but he pretended not to notice, constantly making excuses about being tired from work. He got most of the information about her wellbeing from Dwayne, and many days went by with no sign of her husband returning. So he stopped worrying about her and never acted on Judith's advice. She had said to go in with both feet and see how things work out. But Tucker didn't think he or Catherine were ready for a new love adventure, especially not Catherine. He successfully avoided the woman and her son for a few days until Dwayne asked him the obvious.

"What's wrong with you?" Dwayne brought up the subject on the drive from his new school. Tucker had a day off and swung by that afternoon to pick Dwayne up so they could go grocery shopping together.

"You like her, so why are you avoiding her?" Dwayne pressed, not bothered by Tucker's warning frown.

"What do you know about liking a girl?" Tucker mocked.

Dwayne puffed, then exhaled imaginary smoke.

"Are you smoking?" Tucker asked, taking his eyes off the road for a second.

"Obviously," Dwayne replied and did the puff again.

Tucker growled at Dwayne and snatched the imaginary cigarette from his hand.

"Hey, give me that," Dwayne screamed.

Tucker couldn't help laughing at their private silliness and was glad to see Dwayne sulking.

"Well, we're not changing the subject," Dwayne said.

Tucker played dumb. "What's the subject?"

"The subject is you not being man enough to tell Catherine you love her."

Tucker let out a wild chuckle. "I don't love that woman," he finally said after rubbing tears that came from the corner of his eyes.

"Liar!" Dwayne said.

"Well, stay out of my business, boy. Or I'll be forced to feed you to the lions at the zoo."

Dwayne scoffed at the lame threat and muttered a few words Tucker could barely hear, but there were some he could make out. Love. Pretending. Scared. Steal. Her. Excuses. Chicken.

Tucker shot Dwayne glances every time the teenager muttered a word he could understand.

They got home and Dwayne got out of the car, leaving Tucker behind to bring in the groceries by himself.

"Hey!" Tucker called.

Dwayne didn't look back, but walked away defiantly.

Tucker locked the car and with the groceries in hand, went after Dwayne.

"What's your problem?" he asked the young man as he placed the keys on the kitchen table. They both ignored Dunk, who was in a playful mood and was trying desperately to get Dwayne's attention.

"Just tell her!"

"I can't! Don't you see?"

"I can't believe with all that military muscle, you're afraid of a woman."

Tucker sat and turned on the TV. "Well, every true soldier will tell you that the one person to be very afraid of is a woman," he said.

Dwayne shook his head and walked to where Tucker was sitting before taking a seat next to him.

"Let me teach you something, soldier," Dwayne said.

Tucker laughed. "You're going to teach me. Okay, this should be good."

Dwayne snapped his fingers to get Tucker's attention and Tucker shot him a half-amused, half-contempt look.

"A woman needs for you to show her care, you know. She's delicate. She needs you to pay attention."

Tucker stared at Dwayne as the young man continued to talk.

"Help her around the house, do her chores, cook for her."

Tucker's face showed no emotion. "No," he said and went back to watching the TV.

"It'll do wonders for you. Try it," Dwayne said, sure of himself.

"Nah," Tucker replied.

"But you know I'm telling the truth."

"I don't know any such thing. And if you like her so much, why don't you do her chores?"

Dwayne paused for a second and then shook his head. "Ignore him, Dwayne," he said aloud to himself.

Tucker switched the channel to a football game.

Dwayne wasn't backing down.

"Take her out and without Jerry this time," he said.

Tucker turned down the volume of the TV. "You think I should? Will you watch Jerry while we're gone?" he asked.

"Absolutely. Ten bucks an hour is all it'll cost you."

Tucker laughed hard. "You're a fraudster, kid."

Dwayne ignored him and waved his hands in the air, dismissing the comment. "And I recommend you help with her chores, you know, be handy around the house like I am," he said.

Tucker laughed again. "I'm not helping with her chores."

Dwayne hunched his shoulder and threw his arms in the air.

Tucker laughed once more at the incredibly smart teenager.

"Hey, go sort out the groceries and put them away," Tucker said authoritatively. He knew it upset Dwayne when he played boss with him.

"Yeah, I'll get the groceries. Bla bla bla," Dwayne grumbled.

When Tucker returned home that evening, he met Catherine in his apartment alone.

"Where's everybody?" he asked.

Catherine looked different. She was in a little gown that messed with Tucker's mind ruthlessly.

"Hi, Tucker." She smiled, seated on the couch.

"Hi, Cathy, I'm sorry. Forgive my manners," he said in a soft tone. He didn't know what she was doing.

"Where's everyone?" he asked again.

"My apartment," she answered.

"Alright," Tucker said. He wasn't sure if he was supposed to ask her what she was doing in his apartment or sit down or keep standing.

"I have to go to the bathroom?" he said and dashed off without waiting for a response.

What is she doing?

He considered the possibilities. Was she trying to seduce him? Tucker laughed. No, Catherine was not the type. If she just came to talk, why was everyone else, including Dunk, out of the house? Tucker calmed himself and returned to the living room.

"Have you had dinner?" Catherine asked as soon as he returned. "Well, I made something for—"

"Catherine," Tucker said the minute he could distract himself from her beautiful body. "What are you doing here?"

Catherine stood. "Tucker," she started.

He felt his heart miss a beat.

"Why are you avoiding me?" she continued.

Tucker exhaled. He dug his hands in his pockets and sniffed. He decided to be straight with her. "I don't want to get hurt," he said.

"Is that what you think of me?"

"No, it's not about you."

"Who is it about?"

Tucker removed his hands from his pockets and approached her. "Sit down, Cathy."

Catherine sat on the couch and Tucker followed suit.

"I barely even know you. You don't know me. You're married. You may still love your—"

"I'm not in love with Ray, not anymore."

"That's his name?"

"Yes. It's been seven months."

"Then sign the divorce papers."

"He's threatening me! My son!"

Tucker paused.

"So what are you going to do?"

"Sign the papers, eventually. I don't have enough money to pay a lawyer."

Tucker considered for a minute and nodded, as if to say it's alright. "I want to take care of you," he confessed. "But if you burn me, I don't know how I'd survive."

Catherine took his hand. "Give us a chance, Tucker."

He raised her hand to his lips and kissed it tenderly. He realized at that point how much he wanted a woman to call his own.

Both feet, Tucker, he remembered Judith's advice. He kissed the other hand and looked straight into her eyes. "Alright," he gently said.

Catherine smiled and nodded.

Jake nearly tripped and fell into the swimming pool when Tucker showed up at the gym the next morning with Catherine.

"Shut up, Jake," Tucker cautioned when Jake was about to exclaim in surprise. "She's my neighbor and a good friend."

Jake laughed. "I bet. Who you think you talking to? You think you can lie to me? I know these things! I've been married many years!" he said.

Tucker had expected Jake to be surprised, but he was just overreacting.

"Stop the drama, Jake, and tell me about how my babe is doing."

"Man, Rebecca's doing great, but don't try'n change the subject. What's really going on with you and ya girl?"

"She's not my girl, Jake—"

Jake interrupted him again with another wild laughter.

"Why are you making so much noise?" Tucker said.

Jake paused. "Oh, I'm making too much noise?" He brought out his phone. "Wait till I tell Mom and Becca about this. Oh, and Micah too," he added. "Now, take me to her, would you?"

Tucker considered for a few seconds and resigned. He turned toward Catherine, and Jake followed him with a goofy grin.

"Uh, Cathy, this is my—"

"Cathy, hi," Jake said while offering a handshake. "I'm Jake, his annoying brother. I'm sure you've heard a lot about me."

Catherine laughed and took Jake's hand. "It's a pleasure to meet you, Jake," she replied.

"The pleasure is all mine," Jake said, still wearing his goofy grin.

"You have a really practical gym here."

"Ah, we aim to please, mademoiselle."

Tucker's eyebrows rose. "Since when do you speak French, Jake?"

Jake cocked his head. "Since now, yeah, and I wasn't talking to you."

Catherine laughed while sharing her gaze with Tucker and Jake.

Tucker and Catherine slipped away to the treadmills when a staff member distracted Jake. Catherine smiled nearly the entire workout. The energy she brought impressed Tucker. She admitted she hadn't been to a gym in many years, and he promised she'd become a regular.

After Tucker gave Jake a stern warning to keep his mouth shut about Catherine, the couple left the gym. Before showering and changing their clothes, Tucker showed her a few self-defense moves and asked her to practice on him. He wanted to teach her a few key areas to strike a man in case her husband showed up when he wasn't around. Refining the principle that Officer Rowney taught him when he was younger, Tucker taught Catherine the SING method of defense: solar plexus, instep, nose, and groin. She caught on really fast.

"I always wanted to be a cop, you know," Catherine told him as they finished their session.

"What? Why didn't you go for it?" Tucker asked.

Catherine shrugged. "I don't know," she said while shaking her head. "It's something you want when you're younger, but before you know it, time passes and you're divorced with a kid."

"But are you happy with your life right now?" Tucker asked.

"As a schoolteacher? Yes, I'm happy," she answered.

Tucker believed her. That's what's most important anyway. No matter how life turns out, one is happy in the end. He, of all people, knew that.

———

Early the next morning, Tucker woke to the sound of his phone beeping. He looked at the screen and saw a text message, *I want what's mine.*

"What?" he muttered to himself.

He sat in bed and tapped the phone against the palm of his hand, not sure what to make of the message. After pondering for a few moments, he called Pozo.

"Hey, what's up, man?" Pozo groaned into the phone.

"Sorry to bother you so early in the morning, bro," Tucker said. "But I've been getting some strange text messages."

Pozo sighed. "Strange how?"

"Well, a few days back, I got a call from an unknown number. I ignored the call but got a text immediately after."

"What did the text say?"

"It said, *we'll speak soon.*"

"Hmm, that is strange."

"I know, and just now, I got another saying, *I want what's mine.*"

"I want what's mine?"

"Yeah."

"Have you had any disputes or anything lately?"

Tucker paused for a moment, then shook his head. "No, not that I can think of. And definitely not with someone who'd have my number," he said into the phone.

"Then bro, I'm not sure what to make of any of this," Pozo said. "But it sounds like someone either has the wrong number, is playing games, or really has it in for you."

Tucker nodded at the phone. "Yeah, I agree."

"Just be careful, and I'm right here if you need me, man," Pozo said.

"Thanks bro. I'll keep you informed," Tucker said before ending the call.

He then rested his head on his pillow and thought of Catherine before slowly drifting off to sleep.

The entire day, nothing seemed to go right for Tucker. He felt very uncomfortable and impatient with how his life was moving out of control. He thought about the text messages, and although he knew he'd be safe, he couldn't help but worry about those close to him. Whoever was sending the texts knew things about him and could harm those he cared about.

Tucker's shift ended at nine-thirty that night and it annoyed him. It wasn't the overtime that bothered him because he'd worked plenty of extra hours in the military, but he was supposed to meet with Catherine at nine-thirty and now had to call her to cancel. After informing her, he started for home, angry that he chose that day of all days to go to work without the car.

Tucker left the restaurant and walked across the intersection where he spotted a black mini-van parked at the curb and wondered if it was there a couple of minutes prior or if he was just being paranoid. From his experience, when a soldier smells danger, then danger is probably close by. Tucker walked on and noticed the van inching closer toward him every few steps he took. He was being followed.

He broke into a sprint while dodging around a few pedestrians on the dimly lit, sparsely populated street. He glanced over his shoulder and saw three figures closing in on him, with the van now speeding up as well.

"Great!" Tucker sputtered.

His mind raced as fast as his feet while he decided on what to do next. What they wanted from him was something he would have to figure out later. But at that moment, he needed to escape, so he ran into a dark alley. The men followed him inside and Tucker dealt a kick to the ribs of one of them. The man fell to the ground and writhed in pain. Tucker took his gun and shot at the other two figures following him. He saw one drop to the ground while the other retreated. Tucker raced out of the alley and toward his place.

As he made it closer home, he avoided the main road and stayed out of sight before arriving at his apartment building. He went to the rear of the building and found the maintenance ladder that was stationed near the back of Catherine's place. Tucker unlocked the latch, quickly climbed up, and reached for the window. It was stuck, and the lights were off, which was odd. Tucker hit the window with his elbow and flung it open.

As he landed in the room, he heard a sharp scream and felt something heavy strike the back of his head, and his vision went black.

CHAPTER
ELEVEN

The lights flicked on and Tucker saw Catherine and Dwayne looking down at him with wide eyes and mouths open.

"Oh my God, Tucker, wake up," Catherine said.

"Clay, are you alright, man?" Dwayne asked.

Tucker held the back of his head as he regained his composure from the hit. He signaled for them to be quiet as he dragged himself over to the couch and rested his head.

"Wh—what did you hit me with?" he said with a groan.

"I'm sorry, you scared me. I didn't know it was you," Catherine explained, short of breath.

Tucker squinted and shook his head before briefly placing the index finger of his free hand over his lips. "Arrgh!" he groaned.

Dwayne held him up and attempted to rub the back of his head. Tucker continued to groan.

"I'm so sorry," Catherine cried. "I'm so sorry."

"Get me some water," Tucker said, resting his forehead in his palms.

Dwayne fetched a small glass of water, and Tucker downed it with one gulp.

"More," Tucker said.

Dwayne ran off to get another. "What's going on?" he asked as he came back with another glass.

Tucker swallowed all the water, exhaled, then took in a deep breath. "One more, Dwayne," he said as he gave the teenager back the glass.

Dwayne went to get more water.

"Tucker, what happened?" Catherine asked impatiently.

Tucker looked around. "Where's Jerry?" he asked.

"Asleep, and Dunk is asleep too," Dwayne told him, handing over another glass of water.

Tucker nodded and took in another deep breath.

"Some men were chasing me."

"What?" Dwayne said.

"Oh my goodness!" Catherine put her hands over her mouth. "Who are they?"

"I don't know, but whoever they are, they've been stalking me for days."

Catherine knelt by him. Dwayne followed suit.

"Are they going to come here?" she asked.

Tucker shook his head, uncertain. "I don't know, but I have to be prepared and keep all of you safe. You have to stay in my apartment tonight, Catherine. You can stay in my room with Jerry. Dwayne and I will keep watch."

Tucker fully recovered after a couple of minutes. He walked to the window, shut the blinds, and secured the lock.

Catherine was quiet and Tucker noticed she was shivering. He walked over to calm her.

"Look, Cathy," he said, while resting his hand on her shoulder. "Nothing's gonna happen to you, I promise."

She nodded.

"And you too, Dwayne," Tucker said.

Dwayne sat in a chair, fiddling with a ball-point pen. "Yeah, I know, but I don't want anything to happen to you," he said.

Tucker stared at the young man for a moment before

nodding. "Let's go to my apartment now," he instructed everyone.

"I'll get Jerry," Catherine said.

Tucker took Jerry from Catherine and told her to grab a few extra blankets.

"Let's go," Tucker said while leading them out.

They hurried to his apartment and he bolted the door.

"We'll be safe here. Make sure you don't leave this room unless I say so."

He helped Catherine and Jerry settle in his room, then he and Dwayne camped in the living room. Dwayne was full of questions when they were alone.

"Do you think it has something to do with you being in the military?" Dwayne asked quietly.

Tucker nodded. "You've always been a smart head, Dwayne. I think it may," he said.

"But who could it be, and what do they want from you now?"

"Don't worry your head so much, kid. I got this," Tucker reassured. "Have you had dinner yet?"

"Catherine made chicken soup for us."

"Okay," Tucker said while nodding.

He walked to the kitchen and removed a phone from the cabinet and dialed Pozo's number.

Dwayne winced. "You keep a phone in the cabinet?"

"Ssshhh…" Tucker signaled for Dwayne to be quiet.

"What's up, bro?" Pozo said through the phone after multiple rings. "Our secure phones. This must be serious."

"Someone really has it in for me. At least four men came after me tonight," Tucker said.

"What! Are you—you okay?"

"Yeah, I'm fine."

"So, four of them, huh?"

"Right. Three on foot and at least one more driving a van. I did manage to shoot one of them," Tucker said.

Pozo was quiet for a moment. "I don't know, bro. That's too organized for someone just having it in for you. It's like they want you out of the way, but who?" he said.

"Yeah, I don't know, man," Tucker said.

"I'm here if you need me, bro. Start taking the necessary precautions. Be careful, and you better call me to let me know what I can do to help. You know I'm the one who always saves your butt," Pozo told him.

Tucker chuckled. "Thanks, Pozo," he said before ending the call. "Not a word about this to Catherine," he warned Dwayne.

"Of course," the teenager said.

Tucker stayed awake while everyone else fell asleep. He looked out of the window several times to scan the area before turning to his thoughts for solace as he tried to figure out what to do next.

The first thing on his mind was keeping his family safe. His family. He meant Catherine, Dwayne, Jerry and Dunk. They were not officially a family, but Tucker was comfortable using the word. Who knew? He had loosened up a lot since Catherine waited up for him in his apartment the other night. He had to admit, her beauty and intelligence got him to let his guard down.

He remembered Mr. Rowney telling him frequently that a woman was the most powerful weapon in the hands of an enemy? Well, this woman was a good enemy. He liked the fact she was after his heart. *There's no way I'm letting anything happen to her.*

Tucker looked at Dwayne. He also had to keep him safe. He wasn't taking any chances with Jerry either, or with Dunk. Tucker knew it'd be best to take them all someplace safe, but where exactly, he didn't know.

Dad, I need you now. My life is in danger, and I don't know who's coming after me.

He thought of many more scenarios and what he'd

possibly do. What if it was his past catching up with him? The days when he was a notorious street boy and stole from people. *I'm being paranoid.*

He shook his head. No, he wasn't being paranoid. *I have to keep them safe.*

It was all Tucker could think about. He gathered the box Mr. Rowney had left him and opened it, hoping he'll find something useful.

He stuck his hand inside among the pieces of paper, and the note he drew from the box sent chills through his body.

If all else fails, use violence.

"Music to my ears. Thanks, Dad," Tucker said to himself as he opened a can of soda and gulped it down.

The next morning, Tucker ensured Catherine's apartment windows were secure, and she went back home.

"Just keep them down for now, please," he pleaded with her.

He didn't allow Dwayne to go to school that day because he wanted to ensure the teenager's safety. He figured if they knew where he worked, what time his shift began and ended, then they'd know where he lived and who he cared about. Dwayne was an easy target and Tucker didn't want to take any chances. He made sure he explained everything to Dwayne and was glad the young man understood what was at stake.

Another text came through that morning saying, *YOU'RE DEAD,* but Tucker had stopped being bothered by the text, and for the first time, he replied with: *SO ARE YOU.*

On his way to his bathroom, Tucker heard a noise from Catherine's apartment. Without thinking, he grabbed a knife from the kitchen counter and told Dwayne to stay low. Her door was open a slit, and when Tucker opened it completely, he saw Catherine's ex-husband standing over her as she lay on the rug.

"Get away from her," Tucker demanded.

Ray turned around and looked at Tucker. "Oh?" He cocked his head. "This is the guy?"

Catherine's breathing became heavy, but she said nothing.

Dwayne stepped in and shut the door behind himself.

Ray smirked. "Which one of them are you fooling with, uh?" he asked, his face puckered and his nose crinkled as if he smelled something rotten.

"Not only are you a dog, you look like one," Dwayne spat.

"And you smell like a skunk." Ray laughed. "Oh Catherine, these are your defenders?"

Tucker felt heat rise in his gut, and his sights narrowed on Ray. "Get out of here and don't come back," he said, gritting his teeth on every word.

"Who's gonna make me?" Ray growled. "It's you who should stay out of my wife's life."

Tucker swiftly moved toward Ray and grabbed his collar. "Look, I'll give you one last chance to leave or I'll make you," he said sternly.

Ray pushed against Tucker's chest.

The ex-soldier returned a punch to his attacker's stomach, causing the suited man to bend over in pain. Ray recovered and threw a jab, but Tucker hit him in his eye before he could fully extend his arm.

"That's for hitting my son the other day," Tucker said before punching Ray again. "Now go and don't come back. Sign the papers and leave this woman alone or you'll have me to contend with," Tucker said, delivering a final jab to his upper lip.

Dwayne opened the door, and Ray fled after giving Catherine a threatening look.

Tucker was still fuming. "Did he hurt you?" he asked Catherine.

She shook her head.

"Stay with her, Dwayne," Tucker instructed.

"Where are you going?" Catherine asked.

"I'll be back," Tucker said on his way out the door.

He raced downstairs, out of the apartment building, and towards Ray as the man opened his car door. Tucker pushed the door closed, then grabbed Ray by the collar and shoved him against the car.

"One more finger on that woman and you're dead. Make the divorce final. You have two days," he said.

"Yeah-yeah-yeah, sure, whatever, man," Ray said with his hands in the air.

Tucker released his grip, and Ray fumbled with the door before hopping inside the car and peeling off.

Tucker went to his apartment to wash his bloodied knuckles. He was not in moral doubt about what he had done. For when all else fails, violence would work.

Tucker looked at his reflection in the mirror and calmed his mind. There was a fight coming, and he didn't know who the enemy was, but he knew the smell of danger and could tell that something was about to go down. He rested over the sink in his thoughts. He didn't have any weapons at home and needed to get in touch with Pozo to come up with a plan. After washing the final stain of blood off his skin, Tucker changed out of his sweat-soaked shirt.

Over the few hours that followed, he told Catherine to stay in her apartment with Jerry until he figured out what to do while Dwayne relaxed on the couch and watched a movie.

After Tucker called the restaurant to inform them he wouldn't be in because of a family emergency, he plopped on his bed and took a nap. He had slept for only two hours the previous night. In the military, that would've been the norm for days, but he wasn't used to it anymore.

Tucker woke to his house phone ringing. He wondered where Dwayne was before walking to the living room and seeing the teenager asleep on the couch. Dunk stood in the middle of the room, softly meowing.

"Who's this?" Tucker asked into the phone.

"Your grandfather is dead," a man's voice said.

Tucker flinched. "What! Excuse me, who is—"

The call ended. Tucker dialed the number back immediately, but he got a busy tone. He called his grandfather's line and it was busy too.

"No!" Tucker hit the wall with his fist, causing Dwayne to jump from sleep.

"Hmmmmphrrrr!" Tucker groaned while strangling a kitchen towel. The strangling proved impossible, so he flung the towel across the room.

"Get a change of clothes, Dwayne. We're leaving," he told the startled young man.

"Where're we going?" Dwayne asked.

"You'll be safe at my mother's place."

Dwayne asked no more questions and immediately began packing.

Tucker felt his chest burn with anger and rage. With a long-drawn groan, he pulled his front door open to find Catherine standing there, about to knock and with some papers in her hand.

He ignored the awkward moment and drew her in. "I was coming to talk to you, Catherine," he said.

"Yeah, me too," she replied.

Tucker paused. She wore an indignant look that he had never seen before.

"What's up?" he asked, pacing the floor.

Catherine threw the papers in his face, and he caught a sheet without breaking eye contact with her.

"Catherine," he fussed as he read the sheet of paper.

Dwayne stood frozen, even Dunk was quiet.

"Catherine," Tucker repeated in a gentle tone. "I can explain. Let me explain."

Catherine trembled, then her eyes watered and her lips parted. "The time for explaining has gone!" she yelled before storming toward the door.

Tucker grabbed her, then turned her around so they were face to face.

"Let go of me now!" she said.

Tucker released her. Catherine stared at him for a moment before shaking her head and leaving the apartment.

Dwayne's eyes were wide. "What's wrong with her?" he asked.

Tucker took in a deep breath, then sighed. "She found out some stuff about me. It was a letter from her ex. He dug into my past and found some dirt on me."

"Dirt? What kind of dirt?" Dwayne asked.

"I went to juvie once for battery."

Dwayne winced. "You assaulted someone when you were younger?" he said.

Tucker took in a deep breath. "Listen, I was sixteen. The man was trying to assault a girl and I saw it. I don't know how old the girl was, maybe about twelve. But she was in a dark alley with a grown man and he was trying to take advantage of her," Tucker explained.

Dwayne's chest heaved up and down as he listened.

"I attacked him and beat him really bad. The girl ran off and I was arrested by the cops. They refused my story and said I was trying to mug him."

Dwayne's eyebrows rose. "So they sent you to juvie?"

"Two years," Tucker said. "I'm not proud, but I saved a girl."

Dwayne looked at Tucker.

"Do you believe me?" Tucker asked.

"Yes," Dwayne answered firmly.

Tucker nodded.

"Listen, we have to go. That call was about my grandfather; I think whoever was after me has gotten to him. I have to get there and find out what's going on. Take the phone in the cabinet and don't let it out of your sight. My number's programmed in it."

Dwayne nodded, and Tucker scooped him into a firm hug. After their embrace, Dwayne went to pack while Tucker grabbed some cash from the safe in his bedroom, and then called Pozo.

"Talk to me, brother," Pozo answered the phone.

"I need your help."

"Okay, tell me what you need."

"I just got a call."

"From the same people?"

"I'm certain, but this time they called my house and said Pops is dead."

The line went silent for a moment.

"It could be a trick. Have you tried calling your grandfather?" Pozo asked.

"Got a busy tone."

"What do you need me to do?"

"I have to go check on him and I'm dropping Dwayne off at my mom's. I need you to take Catherine and Jerry someplace safe."

"Wouldn't it be better if she went with you now?"

"It would, but it's complicated."

"Alright. She's still just across the hall from you, right?"

"Yes."

"Okay, I'm on my way."

"Thanks, I owe you," Tucker said.

"I gotcha, bro," Pozo said before ending the call.

Tucker packed a small bag for himself while Dwayne put Dunk in a fresh box, and within seven minutes, they were ready. Tucker turned off everything in his apartment and they went to Catherine's.

She refused to open the door despite Tucker's plea and explanation that she was not safe.

"I've been safe here for a long time," she said to him through the door. "Then you show up and I have to run from my own home?"

The words stung, but Tucker brushed it off.

"I'll leave a number under your doormat, Cathy. It's my friend, Pozo. He'll take you and Jerry someplace safe. Please."

There was no answer.

"Please, Catherine," Tucker leaned against the door.

"Okay," she answered, with the door still locked.

"Get ready now; he's on his way," Tucker said before placing a piece of paper with Pozo's number on it under her doormat.

Tucker drove fast, alert and checking to see if they were being followed. He had the windows up and ensured Dunk was secure in his box.

"What's your mom like?" Dwayne asked.

"She's an angel," Tucker answered. "You'll love her," he added.

Dwayne nodded.

"So what's the plan? How long are you gonna be gone for?" Dwayne asked further.

"What, you miss me already?" Tucker said.

Dwayne smiled for the first time since the previous night and Tucker felt a knot dissolve in his chest.

"I'll be gone for as long as I need to, but just long enough to find out what's going on," he explained.

Dwayne nodded. "Will Catherine be alright?" he asked.

Tucker swallowed down the guilt he felt for putting Catherine in danger and then leaving her at her apartment alone. He should have broken the door down and dragged her with him. "As long as she goes with Pozo. He's ex-military like me and will keep her safe," he answered.

Dwayne nodded again, then fell asleep shortly after.

Tucker parked the car two blocks away from the Rowney's and took Dwayne and Dunk through a series of corners to ensure they weren't being followed.

"We're clear," Tucker told Dwayne. They arrived at the house and entered through the back. It startled Judith to see the trio approach from the back of the house.

"Clarence!" she said.

"Mom," Tucker said as he embraced her. "Calm down, it's fine."

She pursed her lips and shook her head for a moment. "What's going on?" she asked as she looked at Dwayne. "Is this Dwayne?"

Dwayne smiled at her.

"Yep, this is him, and in the box is our cat, Dunk."

Judith offered them seats. "Come, sit," she said.

"Sit over there, Dwayne," Tucker said. "Mom, I need to talk to you. Are the others here?"

Judith held Tucker's hand in hers and led him to Mr. Rowney's old study.

"Talk to me, son. Everyone else is at work, by the way."

"Alright, so I have someone on my tail. I don't know who, but Pops is unreachable, and I need to get to him."

Judith was frowning as Tucker explained. "Strange," she muttered.

"Please look after Dwayne and the cat for me. I'll be back once it's all over."

Judith held his face. "You stay safe, son," she said. "That's an order."

"Of course." Tucker kissed her hand. "Please be safe, too. And don't worry about Dwayne, he's a good kid."

"Of course, son."

"I'll call you."

The meows of Dunk floated to their ears as they left the study.

"The cat eats like crazy, Mom," Tucker said.

Judith laughed.

Tucker hugged Dwayne one last time.

"Stay safe," Dwayne said, burying his head in Tucker's chest.

"I will. Mom will take care of you."

Judith allowed Dwayne to pull away before hugging Tucker herself.

"I love you, Mom."

"I love you too, son," she said.

Tucker peeked out the back door and inspected around the house before racing back to the car and settling behind the wheel. As he jabbed the key into the ignition, his phone rang with Pozo's number on the display.

"Hey man, is she safe?" Tucker asked.

"Bro, she wasn't at the apartment," Pozo said.

"What?" Tucker's heart leapt in his chest.

"She was gone before I got there. Everything looked alright, but she left a note for you."

Tucker took in a deep breath. He figured she'd behave foolishly at some point. Weren't all women like that? So he went to juvie and didn't tell her, but all he had been to her was good. Alright, he was wrong, but she didn't even give him a chance to explain.

"What did the note say?"

"Don't look for me, I'm safe," Pozo said.

"That's all?"

"Yeah."

"Alright, thanks man," Tucker said before ending the call.

"One task at a time, Clarence Tucker," he said to himself when he thought about staying behind to make sure Catherine was safe.

And besides, Pozo would do anything to make sure his girl was fine. With that reassurance, Tucker started the car and sped off for Madro.

Tucker pushed eighty miles per hour the entire drive and made it to Madro in half the time it'd normally take. He had tried his grandfather's line several times during the trip and couldn't get through. He remained calm and prepared for the worst as he pulled up to the house and exited the car with his head on a swivel.

Tucker found the front door open and went inside. His grandfather was sitting at the table in front of an empty plate, wiping his mouth with a napkin.

"Pops," Tucker said as he checked around the house.

The old man's eyes widened, and his mouth fell open. "Clarence! Whatta lovely surprise!"

Tucker's forehead wrinkled, and he sighed and shook his head before sitting at the table with his grandfather. "Pops, are you alright? Did someone try to hurt you? Is there a problem?" he asked while craning toward the old man.

"Problem? Not at all, perfectly alright."

Tucker sat up, still unsure about what was happening. "Someone called me this morning, a man. He said you were in danger."

Pops frowned. "That's really strange. Everything here's

perfect," he said. "Except for the phone lines being down—and I got a call from a maintenance man not to worry about that."

Tucker sat back and exhaled. He closed his eyes and groaned, trying to figure out why someone would want to lure him away from New York.

"Mom," he whispered.

"What?"

"I have to go look for Marie," Tucker said, standing and making his way toward the front door.

Pops tried to stand up. "Er, okay, son, be careful," he called after him.

Tucker dashed from the house, jumped in the car, then drove to her restaurant and walked up to the front desk.

"Hi, is Marie here?" he asked.

The waiter on duty frowned.

"I'm sorry," Tucker said, shifting his weight from one foot to the other. "I'm Clarence. She knows me—I'm here to see her."

The waiter shook his head. "Boss hasn't been here today. You can talk to the manager."

Tucker turned in the direction the server pointed and saw a middle-aged man walking toward him. Tucker hurried to the man.

"I'm Clarence, Marie's son. I just learned she hasn't shown up for work today," he said to the heavy-built man.

The man looked surprised. Tucker figured it was the first the man had heard of Marie having a son.

"Yes," he said in a heavy British accent. "And not answering her phone, either."

Tucker immediately backed away. "Thank you," he said as he ran outside.

He was at Marie's house in what seemed like two seconds, dashing out of the car with speed.

He found the front door unlocked and entered. The scent

of sauteed spices and seasonings stuffed the house. The furniture in the living room sat organized and neat, and the sound of a pot's lid rattling under the pressure of steam flowed from the kitchen. Tucker entered the kitchen and saw the pot on the stove and chopped vegetables on the counter, but didn't see Marie.

"Mom," he called. "Where are you?"

No answer. Tucker walked to the back door, and just when he reached for the handle, it swung open and Marie stepped inside with a bowl in her hand.

"Aah! Clarence, son," she said, while placing her free hand on her chest. "You scared me."

"Are you okay?" Tucker asked.

She winced as she shut the door behind herself. "Yes, I'm fine," she said with a chuckle. "Except for you tryna' give me a heart attack," Marie continued while walking past Tucker and placing the bowl on the counter.

"I stopped by the restaurant. They said you didn't show up and weren't answering your phone."

"Yeah, that's because I'm taking some time off and making your grandfather a meal. The manager can handle things at the restaurant. What's with you?"

"Something's goin' on. Can you finish cooking over at Pop's house?"

Marie hunched her shoulders. "I'm sure I can. Just need to bring the ingredients, but what's going on?"

"I'll explain on the way. Get what you need and some change of clothes for tonight."

Tucker parked in front of his grandfather's house and gestured for his mother to wait inside the car. The front door was open, and as he approached, he heard Pop's voice.

"Clarence, that's you?"

Tucker exhaled a breath he didn't realize he was holding. "Yeah, it's me. Are you okay, Pops?"

"I'm fine," the old man said as he stood from his chair and walked toward the door.

Tucker walked back to the car and helped Marie carry her things into the house while Pops held the door open.

"What's goin' on?" Pops asked.

"Mom's gonna stay with you while I look into that phone call I got this morning," Tucker said.

Pops squinted.

"She's making you a healthy meal, Pops."

"What?"

Tucker's phone rang. He held up a finger and stepped outside.

"Pozo," he answered.

"How's everything going, bro?"

"Well, both my mother and grandfather are okay."

"That's good. But I wonder why they said your grandfather was dead."

"I'm not sure. It's like they wanted to lure me to Madro for some reason."

"Or away from New York," Pozo said.

"Yeah. Hey, any luck finding Catherine?"

"Not yet."

Tucker exhaled sharply.

"I'll keep looking for her. Leave that to me," Pozo said.

At that, another call came into Tucker's phone.

"Hey man. My mother, Judith, is calling me."

"Alright."

"I'll call you back soon," Tucker said before ending the call with Pozo and answering the call for Judith.

"Mom?" he answered.

"Hi, son. Are you okay? How's your grandfather?"

"I'm fine, and he's fine, too."

"Okay, great. That's a relief. I called to let you know we're leaving the house."

"Leaving? Where? Why?"

"Becca has gone into labor. We're all heading to the hospital. Jake is on his way too."

Tucker groaned and felt his heart beat against his chest, knowing he may miss the baby's birth. "Give her my love, mom," he said.

"Everything will be fine, son. Do what you have to do and come back home to me," Judith said.

"I will. Is Dwayne around?"

"Yeah, I think he stepped outside. I'll go get him."

Tucker kept the phone to his ear as ruffling and static filled the line. He heard a door creak open, followed by Judith's voice.

"Dwayne!" she called out.

More ruffling and static fill the line. This continued another minute before a door shut and Judith's voice came back on the line.

"I'm not sure where he went. He was just outside."

Tucker sighed. "He does that sometimes."

"What?"

"Disappear without telling you where he's going."

"Reminds me of someone," Judith said with a slight chuckle in her voice.

"No. This boy can be difficult."

"Oh, really?"

Tucker kissed his teeth. "We're not—anyway, he probably went for a walk or something. I'll call him."

"Alright, let me know, son."

"Okay," Tucker said before ending the call.

Tucker dialed the number for the burner phone he had given to Dwayne.

"Mr. Tucker, you're a hard man to reach," a man's deep voice answered.

Tucker squinted. "Who's this? Where's Dwayne?"

The man chuckled. "I go by many names, but you can call me King X. And Dwayne's right here."

"Put 'em on," Tucker demanded.

"Not so fast, soldier."

"If he's hurt—"

"No. He's fine. Now if he stays that way depends on you."

"What do you want?"

"It's simple. Dwayne is… under contract with me. He has work to do—he's one of my soldiers."

"You mean drug dealers?"

"Tomato, tomahto."

"Well, that's not happening. The kid has left the street life behind."

"Oh, you think puttin' the boy into a fancy little school and gettin' him a penny-pinching job is gonna take the street out of 'em?"

"Maybe not, but being with people who love him will."

"Ahh, how touching," King X mocked. "When we found out you was his school's emergency contact, it touched my heart. I think I might've even teared up."

"Look, Dwayne has left that life behind, and all the scum that come with it. Now put 'em on the phone."

"You think ya betta than me? I looked into you, and your past isn't all sparkling clean. So, I suggest you watch what you say, or you may never speak to the boy again."

Tucker inhaled, then slowly exhaled. "What do you want?" he asked.

"I want Dwayne to finish paying off his debts."

"I told you, he's not running anymore."

"That's too bad. I guess I'll need my payment in full, then."

"How much?"

"According to my calculations… one-hundred and fifty thousand should cover it. No, no, no, wait. You shot and injured one of my men, so one-hundred and seventy-five should even us out."

"Why don't you stop this now and just let the kid go? This —it just won't end well for you."

"You have six hours to get me my money. When you have it, call me back and we'll arrange a meet, understand?"

Tucker knew it would be nearly impossible for him to get his hands on that kind of money, but he had to go along for Dwayne's sake.

"Yeah, I understand."

"Good. I'll be—"

"Wait. If you want that kinda money, I need to speak with Dwayne. I need to know he's okay," Tucker said.

King X sighed. "Whateva. Yo Dwayne, ya daddy on the phone. Here."

"Clay," Dwayne said with a sharp exhale.

"Dwayne, are you okay?"

"I'm sorry, man. I went for a walk to clear my head and, they-they grabbed me."

"It's fine, it's fine. Are you hurt?"

"No, I'm—"

"That's enough," King X's voice scorned. "There. Now that you know he's alive, go get my money."

"Are you sure you want to do this?"

"I'm pretty sure. You have five hours and fifty-six minutes."

King X ended the call and Tucker growled and hollered. Marie stepped outside with Pops a few paces behind her.

"What's wrong, Clarence?" she asked.

"What's goin' on, son?" Pops asked.

Tucker knew that King X had no intentions of letting Dwayne or him leave alive. He would have to go into the meet prepared to fight, so getting Marie and Pops involved would do nothing but worry them.

"I have to get back," Tucker said. "You two stay here and I'll call you later."

Tucker dashed toward his car and heard both Maria and Pops shout his name.

"I'll call you later," he said before entering the car.

While driving back into town, Tucker called Judith and told her he had talked to Dwayne and was on his way to get the teenager, so she should take Dunk and head to the hospital to be with Becca. She didn't protest, but told Tucker to be careful. After ending his call with Judith, Tucker dialed Pozo's number.

"What's up, brutha?" Pozo answered. "Still no luck finding Catherine."

"That's fine, bro. I have something more pressing."

"What's that?"

"I found out who's been stalking me."

"Who?"

"A drug dealer who goes by the name King X."

"King X? Who does this guy think he is?"

"Yeah. But Pozo," Tucker said before exhaling.

"What's up?"

"He has Dwayne."

"Ah man."

"I need a plan, and fast."

"Well, what are we waiting for? You're an A-team member. Let's put a plan together. Whatcha say to that?"

"I say this guy doesn't realize what he brought on himself."

Pozo chuckled. "Indeed, amigo. Indeed."

After finishing his conversation with Pozo, Tucker arrived home. While in his apartment, he removed a duffle bag from his closet and stuffed a pair of binoculars, a few paper magazines, pamphlets, and some small books inside before removing his cell phone and tapping a number from his recent calls.

"You got my money," King X answered.

"Yeah, I got it."

"That was faster than I thought it'd be. Maybe the boy does have a—"

"Let's just get on with it," Tucker interrupted. "Where do you wanna meet?"

"Straight to business. Alright. You know where the old Pier four is?"

"The one in Brooklyn?"

"That's the one. There's a hangar. Meet us there in an hour."

"Yeah."

"And Mr. Soldier."

"What?"

"I betta not smell cops. Because if I do, Dwayne goes for a swim."

The phone beeped as the call ended. Tucker gritted his teeth and flung the duffle bag over his shoulder before exiting his apartment and stepping into the hall. He paused and stared at Catherine's apartment door, thinking maybe he should check if she was home. The thought of Dwayne came to his mind as he jolted his head and turned for the stairs. On his way out of the apartment building, Tucker removed his phone and called Pozo's number.

"Yo," Pozo answered.

"I have the location."

Thirty minutes later, Tucker stood at the edge of a canal about two-hundred yards diagonally across from the boat hangar at

Pier four. Behind him sat a couple of empty, old warehouse buildings, and in front of him was the bay. With his binoculars to his eyes, he leaned over the railing and watched as two men circled in front of the hangar. Both had pistols tucked inside their waistbands. He recognized one of the men from the group that chased him the other night. As Tucker removed the binoculars from his face, he heard footsteps approach his side. He turned to find Pozo walking toward him with a duffle bag of his own.

"How are we looking?" Pozo asked.

Tucker glanced at the hangar, then back at Pozo. "I see two men on the parameter. Both armed with handguns. Probably Glocks."

"Interesting. We have Glocks too," Pozo said as he sat his bag on the pavement, squatted, then unzipped it. "Here," he continued as he handed Tucker a Glock 19.

Tucker checked the chamber of the gun, then placed it inside his duffle bag, while Pozo stuffed another Glock in the back of his own waistband.

Pozo reached back inside his bag and produced a hand grenade. "Here's the showstopper," he said as he passed it to Tucker.

Tucker settled the grenade inside a small compartment within his duffle bag. He tied the grenade's pin to a strap attached to the bag.

"Did you bring the rifle, the M200?" he asked.

"Oh, you mean Bertha. Yeah, I have it, and the suppressor." Pozo reached inside his pocket and removed a small, flat case. "Here, take this," he said as he opened the case, exposing two tiny silver buttons. They looked like watch batteries, except they were much smaller. Pozo gave one to Tucker. "Hide it inside your ear," he said.

"I remember these. How do you manage to get your hands on this stuff?" Tucker said while placing the tiny transceiver inside of his ear.

"Well, I… I borrowed these when we had some training at that CIA site in Ankara," Pozo said as he worked his transceiver inside his ear. "And the guns, well, I've always had lots of guns."

Tucker laughed, then looked at his watch. "We have twenty minutes to go," he said.

"Okay, testing, testing. Can you hear me?"

"Loud and clear."

"Okay, I'll cover you from this warehouse. Watch your six, bro," Pozo said before pivoting toward the building.

"Hey, Pozo," Tucker called.

Pozo turned.

"I really—"

"Hey, no need to," Pozo interrupted. "But thank me when it's over," he finished, before dashing toward the warehouse.

Tucker watched his friend disappear inside the building before making his way toward the hangar.

It took him ten minutes to arrive at the concrete deck. The two men near the boat hangar faced him as he approached. One of them had a low-fade, and the other was bald.

Tucker felt a slight vibration in his ear. "I got a clear view of the hangar, so you're covered on the outside," Pozo's voice came through the earpiece.

"Copy that," Tucker said as he thumped across the wooden dock.

When he was ten feet away from the hangar's entry, the bald man stuck one hand out and placed his other hand on the Glock tucked in his front waistband.

"That's far enough," he said, before nodding to his partner, then Tucker. "Put the bag down and raise ya arms."

Tucker did as instructed while the man with the low-fade walked to him and frisked him. As the man passed his hands down Tucker's sides, he leaned to his ear.

"Don't think I forgot about you shooting my partna' the other night."

Tucker exhaled but said nothing.

Once the man finished patting Tucker down, he looked at the bald guy.

"He's clean."

The bald man nodded. "Okay, let's move," he said as he waved them toward the hangar.

Tucker picked up the duffle bag and walked to the entry with the two men a few paces behind him. Water splashed against the dock stilts, and as Tucker entered, he saw Dwayne sitting on a thirty-by-thirty-foot wooden platform with his hands behind his back, and standing next to him, was a tall, muscular man with a gun. On the opposite side of Dwayne, sitting on a bench, was who Tucker guessed was King X. The man wore a full beard, a mini fro, and had a small scar below his right eye.

He stood. "Mr. Soldier," he said while looking at his diamond-filled watch. "You were quick about gettin' my money, and you'a lil early. I like that."

"You're King X?" Tucker asked.

"The one and only," the man said, opening his arms, smiling, and exposing his four gold teeth. "But I'm feeling personable, so I'll allow you to call me Xavier."

"Well, Xavier, I have your money," Tucker said while lifting his duffle bag. "So let the boy go."

"Not so fast. I want to see the money first."

"No. Dwayne goes free first. I want to guarantee his safety."

Xavier scoffed. "Not like ya got a choice," he said. "You're surrounded, outnumbered, and ya already brought the money. You played all ya cards, soldier. Now open the bag, slowly."

The tall guy standing next to Dwayne trained his gun on Tucker.

Looking over his shoulder and seeing the other two men hold their guns to their sides, Tucker suspended the duffle bag in front of himself and unzipped it a slit. He stuck his hand inside, grabbed the grenade, clasped the safety lever, then let the bag drop to the ground along with the grenade pin.

Everyone jumped at the sight of the explosive weapon in Tucker's hand.

"That-that's a grenade," the man with the low-fade said.

The tall guy kept his gun on Tucker, and Dwayne just stared as the situation unfolded.

"Take it easy," Xavier said. "Let's make a deal."

"The deal is simple," Tucker said. "You're gonna untie him, and he's walking outta here. If not, then I guess none of us will be leaving."

Xavier's mouth shrugged.

Tucker extended the grenade toward the kingpin. "Now!" he asserted.

"Boss?" the tall guy said, with his gun still aimed at Tucker.

"Untie him," Xavier said.

The muscular man lowered his gun, removed a small blade, then cut the zip tie that bound Dwayne.

Dwayne walked to Tucker and stood next to him.

"Get out of here," Tucker said.

"What about—"

Tucker bulged his lips, then shook his head and said, "Dwayne—not the time."

The teenager jogged out of the hangar, and Tucker waved the grenade in the air while he squatted to pick up the duffle bag.

"What's your plan now, Mr. Soldier?" Xavier said.

Tucker felt a vibration in his ear.

"I see Dwayne," Pozo said. "And the cops are four minutes out."

Four minutes.

"I'm going outside for some fresh air," Tucker said as he slowly backpedaled toward the door.

"I think we'll join you," Xavier said.

Tucker grinned. "That's up to you." He continued to ease toward the exit with Xavier and the tall, muscular guy in his front and the guy with the low-fade along with his bald partner at his back. The four men had their guns aimed at him and tracked his every movement. When he stepped, they stepped. The water continued to splash, and a fishy stench Tucker didn't notice before wafted in the air. Each of Tucker's steps became heavier than the one before. It felt as if he had bricks for shoes.

As he made it outside of the hangar, his arm tired. The grenade went from weighing five pounds to thirty-five pounds, and his bicep spasmed. When they were near the concrete deck, Tucker stopped and glanced to his left. He saw Dwayne running toward the abandoned warehouses.

Xavier followed Tucker's gaze. "Don't worry about the kid; we'll take care of 'em later," he said. "So, how ya gonna get out of this, soldier?"

Tucker narrowed his sights on the kingpin and continued to step backward.

"I got a clear shot on these clowns," Pozo's voice scratched in Tucker's ear.

Tucker stopped walking. "Hit the two behind me," he said.

"Roger that," Pozo said in his ear.

"Whatchu say, soldier?" Xavier asked as two claps roared and bullets whistling through the air.

The man behind Tucker with the low-fade screamed, dropped his gun, then fell from the deck and toward the water. The bald man dropped his gun and reached for his leg while hollering.

Noticing Xavier and the tall man distracted by the cries of their partners, Tucker swung his duffle bag, knocked the tall guy's gun toward the water, then shoulder-butted him. The muscular man lost his balance and shuffled backward. In the same motion, Tucker spun and elbowed Xavier in the nose, causing the kingpin to spin toward the deck floor and his gun to drop, then splash into the water.

"Your six!" Pozo's voice warned.

"You're dead," the bald guy said.

Tucker turned and saw the man crawling toward his gun. Before the man could grasp his firearm, Tucker raced to him and delivered a football kick to his jaw. The bald guy fell back, then sprawled on the ground, unconscious. When Tucker turned toward Xavier, he saw the kingpin kneeling on the deck and holding his nose. He looked a little farther to the right and saw the tall, muscular man staring at him with bulging eyes, flared nostrils, and gritted teeth. The big guy charged at Tucker. Realizing he was still holding the grenade and duffle bag, Tucker slung the grenade far into the water, dropped the duffle bag, then braced himself for impact.

"Move, so I can get a clear shot," Pozo said as the muscular man tackled Tucker to the ground.

The tall guy sat on top of Tucker with his hands wrapped around his neck. Tucker grabbed for the man's face, but his reach was an inch too short. He then punched the man's sides and arms but couldn't get enough leverage, so his attacks were essentially love taps. As Tucker fought to break the man's grip from around his neck, a loud blast erupted and water rained down on the deck. The man glanced over his shoulder, and Tucker grabbed both of his thumbs and bent them back at the same time. The big guy yelled and loosened his grip. Tucker then clenched the man's wrists and pulled them apart, causing the muscle guy to lean down. When the man's face dropped within Tucker's grasp, he clasped the sides of the man's head and pushed his thumbs into his eyes. Tucker felt the tall man's eyeballs squelch as if they were ready to pop. The man screamed as Tucker forced him off.

Tucker crawled to his feet while the man placed his hands over his eyes and continued to scream.

"I can take him," Pozo said.

"No," Tucker said. "He's mine. Get Dwayne."

Tucker punched the man in the gut, then kicked him twice in the groin. The tall man screams hit a higher pitch than before as he doubled over. Tucker swung and hit him with a right, then a left, and finally a straight right. The man's eyes rolled to the back of his head and he plummeted backward.

As adrenaline shot through his body, Tucker growled at the sky in part rage and part celebration. He heard footsteps behind him and turned to find Xavier running in the same direction as Dwayne. Tucker snatched his duffle bag from the ground and gave chase. Within four seconds, he was three feet away from Xavier. Tucker slung his duffle bag and it smacked into Xavier's back, causing the criminal to stumble and fall to the pavement.

Sirens howled through the sky, and Tucker heaved Xavier from the ground by his collar.

"Where ya goin'?" Tucker said.

Xavier shoved Tucker's chest. "Get off me," he said, breaking free.

The two squared off, and Xavier threw a wild punch at his opponent. Tucker bobbed under the attack, then landed a powerful cross directly to Xavier's jaw. The kingpin dropped to the ground, and Tucker loomed over him as the blare from the sirens drew closer. Xavier stared at Tucker with his eyes bulged, his mouth opened, and short of breath.

"This ends here," Tucker said.

"Look-look man. You don't hafta' do anything crazy. Dwayne's debt's paid in full."

"You right, it is. And if you bother him, or me, or anyone I know ever again," Tucker said before gritting his teeth and shaking his head. "I will kill you." He gave Xavier a cold stare. "Do you understand?"

The criminal slowly nodded.

"Good, and goodnight," Tucker said as he planted his heel in the man's face.

Xavier's head bounced off the concrete, then he fell sound asleep.

The sirens rang louder, and Tucker saw a glimpse of flashing red and blue lights from the corner of his eye. He picked up his duffle bag, then raced toward one of the abandoned warehouses. As Tucker bent a corner at the building, he saw Dwayne squatted in the alleyway.

"I'm sorry, Clay. I didn't—" the teenager started, out of breath.

Tucker quickly embraced him. "It's okay. Let's go."

The two hustled through the alley, threaded through a few buildings, then jogged to the canal where Tucker did his initial reconnaissance. Pozo met them as they arrived.

"Are you guys okay?" he asked, adjusting his duffle bag on his shoulder.

"Yeah, we're fine," Tucker said.

"I'm sorry I was a little late on calling the cops."

Tucker shook his head as he placed his bag on the pavement and removed his binoculars. "It worked out. If you weren't late, I might be in handcuffs right now." Tucker looked through the field glasses and saw three squad cars surrounding Pier Four's hangar. An officer led Xavier to a car in cuffs while other officers fished one of Xavier's men from the water and examined the other two.

Tucker smiled. "Whatta' beautiful sight. I love it when a plan works out," he said, while handing the binoculars to Pozo.

Pozo looked toward the hangar, and Dwayne approached Tucker.

"I'm sorry, man. X is somebody I thought I was done with. They just grabbed me and—" the teenager started.

Tucker placed his hand on the young man's shoulder. "It's

okay," he said. "It's not like you invited them back into your life, unlike someone I know."

Dwayne chuckled. "I learned a lot from that someone."

Tucker took in a breath, then slowly exhaled. "The important thing is that you're okay," he said while grabbing Dwayne's chin and turning the teenager's face to the side. "You have a lil scratch."

"I'm lucky that's all I have."

Tucker nodded, then smiled. The two stared at each other as the waves crashed into the deck wall and the seagulls squawked.

"Well, I did it again," Pozo said as he strutted to Tucker and Dwayne. "Another successful mission under my belt. I'm like a one-man army," he finished before handing Tucker the binoculars.

Dwayne laughed.

Tucker winced. "I'm pretty sure you weren't the one surrounded by four armed men."

Pozo shrugged. "You tell your story, I'll tell mine." He placed his hand on Dwayne's shoulder. "I'm happy you're safe, kid." He glanced at Tucker. "Both of you."

"Thanks," Dwayne said.

"Anytime, but we should probably get a move on it."

Tucker nodded. "You're right. Let's get out of here. Oh!"

Both Pozo's and Dwayne's eyes widened.

"What?" Pozo said.

"I forgot Becca went into labor. I have to get to the hospital."

"Okay, you go. Give me your bag. I'll take care of it."

"Thanks bro," Tucker said before shaking hands with Pozo and pulling him in for an embrace.

"I always got your six."

"And I got yours." Tucker gave Pozo the duffle bag. "Let's go, Dwayne."

. . .

It took Tucker and Dwayne twenty-five minutes to arrive at the hospital. He called Judith on the way and she told him what floor she was on. They took the elevator up, and as the doors dinged open, Judith stood, greeting them with a smile. She grabbed Dwayne and hugged him.

"Are you okay?" she asked.

"I'm-I'm fine," Dwayne said.

Once she released Dwayne, she looked at Tucker.

"Everything's good, Mom," he said.

Judith hugged him. "Okay, you two," she said after their embrace. "Come meet the newest edition to our family."

At that, Tucker's phone rang.

"I better take this," he said. "You two go. I'll catch up."

"Okay," Judith said. "There's a waiting room down the hall."

"Alright."

Tucker walked down the hall while Judith and Dwayne walked in the opposite direction. He heard the two talking over the beeping hospital equipment.

"Where's Dunk?" Dwayne asked.

"Oh, he's downstairs in the pet care center," Judith answered.

When Tucker reached the waiting room, he answered his phone.

"Are you okay?" Marie's voice came through.

"Yes. Everything's fine—everybody's fine."

"Okay, you scared us when you ran off. What happened?"

"Did you get 'em? Is that him on the line now?" Pops asked in the background.

"I'll explain later," Tucker said.

"Is he okay?" Pops asked.

"He's fine," Marie told Pops.

"Okay then, tell him he owes his grandfather a proper visit."

Marie laughed. "You heard that?"

"I did. I'll see you two soon," Tucker said.

"Okay son. Stay safe, and I love you."

"I love you too," Tucker said before ending the call.

He exited the room and walked down the hall toward Judith and Dwayne. The two stood smiling while facing a window. Tucker stepped behind them and looked. On the other side of the window, Jake stood dressed in scrubs, and in his arms squirmed a tiny person with fine hair, smooth skin, and puffy cheeks. The baby's tiny hand reached toward Jake's face.

Judith placed her hands over her mouth. "Ahhh. She's so beautiful," she said.

Jake glanced at Tucker with a smile on his face.

Tucker smiled back. "Adorable," he said.

Judith turned to him. "You're next," she said with a huge smile on her face.

Tucker scoffed. "Yeah right," he said. "Where's Micah?"

"In the room with is Mom and Miriam, asleep."

Tucker nodded, then sighed.

Judith studied his face for a moment. "How's your friend? I still haven't met her yet."

Dwayne glanced at Tucker before turning back to the observation window.

"It's—well, it's a bit complicated at the moment," Tucker told Judith.

Judith placed her hand on his shoulder. "It'll all work out, son," she said.

"Hopefully."

Jake nodded for Judith to enter the nursery, and as she walked toward the door, Tucker stepped next to Dwayne. The teenager hung his head toward the ground.

"You okay?" Tucker asked.

Dwayne looked at him and winced. "Yeah-yeah I'm fine."

"Really? What's on your mind, kid?"

"Nothing. I just… my past could've hurt this family, and if you didn't—"

"That's what family do," Tucker said as he placed an arm around Dwayne. "We protect each other. When one of us hurts, all of us hurt. You understand?"

Dwayne smiled and nodded.

Tucker returned the smile. "Good," he said while facing the window and watching Judith hold her granddaughter for the first time. "Because at the rate this family's growing, it won't be long before you'll have to be there for one of us."

EPILOGUE

Tucker placed a basket of food and a bottle of sparkling grape juice in the back of his car. He slid behind the wheel, started the engine, then bobbed his head to the music blaring from the stereo as he veered onto the road. He had returned Judith's car and purchased a Subaru from a car dealership Pozo recommended.

The thoughts that lingered in his mind all day came back. For the past few days, he felt things were going to change soon and decided to give it one more try. He was prepared, and hopeful, so he picked up his phone and tapped the number.

"Hi," a voice answered.

Tucker cleared his throat and braced himself.

"Cathy, how are you?" he asked.

"Better than you since I don't have to lie about my past."

Tucker sighed into the phone and hoped she heard it.

"I called to say it again, Cathy. I'm sorry. I really am."

Catherine was quiet.

"How's Jerry?" Tucker asked.

"He's good, talks about you a lot, Dwayne and Dunk too."

"See? He misses us," Tucker said, hoping it made

Catherine smile. "I know what I want, and it's you. I want you, all of you. Please, Cathy."

Catherine was quiet.

"I'll think about it," she finally said.

"Please," Tucker said again, expecting her to click off, but she didn't, so he took it as a good sign. It was progress from the last time when she didn't even wait for him to finish.

"If you let me, I promise to be your friend, protector, and lover, because I cherish you that much, Cathy."

"Yeah?" Catherine asked.

"I promise," Tucker affirmed.

She hung up. Tucker took the phone from his ear and looked at his home screen.

It was three weeks since everything happened and he hadn't seen Catherine in that time. He knew he could track her, but he didn't want to invade her privacy.

As he drove home, he decided that if she really thought what he did was worth leaving him, then they were probably better off apart.

He planned to call Jake and Becca first thing when he arrived home, and now that he had committed to going home regularly, he was excited about seeing his niece, Josie.

"Thanks for giving me a family, Officer Rowney," he said aloud, feeling lucky that Judith, Becca, Jake and their children could hardly let him go a week before asking to see him. They were already trying to have him commit to cooking fried chicken for them every Sunday. He had promised he'd think about it. Tucker smiled; just thinking about them comforted him.

After a few moments, he exited his car, hiked to his apartment, unlocked the door, and nudged it, but it wouldn't fully open.

"Who are you?" Dwayne's voice came from the other side of the door.

"Dwayne, if you make me wait one more second—"

The door swung open and Tucker came face to face with Catherine.

Tucker's eyes widened. "Catherine!" he exclaimed.

"Clarence," she said.

Tucker squinted. "What are you doing here?"

"Did you mean what you said?"

"Huh?"

"About cherishing me."

Tucker slowly nodded. "Every word of it," he said.

"You better, because I cherish you too. And I've missed you so much," Catherine said.

She jumped into his arms and he held her while signaling for Dwayne to take the basket out of his hand.

Dwayne grabbed the basket.

Tucker lifted Catherine up, and she curled her legs around him.

Dwayne winced. "I'm still here, guys," he scoffed.

Tucker carried her inside and noticed Jerry aching to jump on his neck.

"Jerry!" Tucker said as he lowered Catherine and caught the boy.

Jerry cackled as Tucker threw him up in the air.

"Higher, Uncle Tuck," he shouted.

Dwayne stood till Tucker was done. "You're gonna hug me too?" he asked.

Tucker threw a pillow at the teenager's head, and they all laughed. He signaled for Dwayne to get lost and the young man responded by rolling his eyes and taking Jerry with him in the room.

"I'm sorry about everything, Cathy," Tucker said when they were alone.

"You don't have to explain. Dwayne told me everything," Catherine replied.

Tucker kissed her hand.

Catherine closed her eyes briefly and sighed. "I just hate

secrets, Tucker," she said while shaking her head. "That's what crushed my marriage. Ray kept a lot of secrets from me."

Tucker pursed his lips and glanced at the floor.

"I was beginning to think maybe it's my fault that the only two men I've ever loved kept their pasts from me," she went on.

Tucker raised her hand to his lips and pressed it in.

"I've signed the divorce papers. Turns out it wasn't money I needed," she said.

"What did you need?"

Catherine looked at him. "Someone to show me I wasn't alone," she said.

Tucker nodded and used her finger to trace his lips. "I have a question for you," he said.

Catherine nodded. "What is it?" she asked with a smile.

"Have we kissed before?"

She giggled. "Maybe in our dreams."

"Right," Tucker said. "Well, let me make it our reality."

Before she could reply, he landed his lips squarely on hers and held her firmly in place. Catherine closed her eyes, and Tucker felt her heart racing. When he released her, she blushed and a tear lingered in the corner of her right eye.

"I love you," Tucker whispered in her ear.

She smiled. "I love you too."

"My mother's dying to meet you," Tucker said.

Catherine giggled.

"So is mine, soldier," she replied, her eyes dancing with delight.

ENJOYED THIS BOOK?

I have a favor to ask. If you have a moment, I would really appreciate it if you could leave a short review on the page where you purchased this book. I'm thankful for you sharing your feedback about this book. It really helps new readers find this series.

Sign up for notifications of new books by Alex Cage and exclusive giveaways

www.AlexCage.com/signup

ALSO BY ALEX CAGE

If you liked Clarence Tucker, you'll love Orlando Black and Leroy Silver. Grab your next adventure today!

Orlando Black Series

Carolina Dance (Novel)

Queen City Ruby (Short Story)

Sunshine Scandal (Short Story)

Once You Go Black (Short Story)

Bayside Boom (Novel)

Family Famous (Novella)

Leroy Silver Series

Contracts & Bullets

Aloha & Bullets

Get the latest releases and exclusive giveaways, sign up to the Alex Cage Reader List.

www.AlexCage.com/signup

ABOUT THE AUTHOR

Alex Cage is an action adventure thriller author.

Cage's books blend his interest in martial arts, adventure, travel, and knowledge with exploration and high-octane action. Cage enjoys action adventure and thriller stories with fantasy and sci-fi sprinkled in. He has always wanted to create his own stories but spent many years thinking about it before actually putting his stories on paper. He currently lives in North Carolina where he enjoys reading, writing, and practicing martial arts.

Cage always loves to hear from his readers, so feel free to contact him:

www.alexcage.com
connect@alexcage.com

www.ingramcontent.com/pod-product-compliance
Lightning Source LLC
Chambersburg PA
CBHW031020190726

48286CB00003BA/939